OTHER YEARLING BOOKS YOU WILL ENJOY:

BABE, THE GALLANT PIG, *Dick King-Smith*
HARRY'S MAD, *Dick King-Smith*
MARTIN'S MICE, *Dick King-Smith*
PEARL'S PROMISE, *Frank Asch*
PEARL'S PIRATES, *Frank Asch*
QUENTIN CORN, *Mary Stolz*
THE CRICKET IN TIMES SQUARE, *George Selden*
HARRY CAT'S PET PUPPY, *George Selden*
HARRY KITTEN AND TUCKER MOUSE, *George Selden*
HENRY, *Nina Bawden*

YEARLING BOOKS/YOUNG YEARLINGS/YEARLING CLASSICS are designed especially to entertain and enlighten young people. Patricia Reilly Giff, consultant to this series, received the bachelor's degree from Marymount College. She holds the master's degree in history from St. John's University, and a Professional Diploma in Reading from Hofstra University. She was a teacher and reading consultant for many years, and is the author of numerous books for young readers.

For a complete listing of all Yearling titles,
write to Dell Readers Service,
P.O. Box 1045,
South Holland, IL 60473.

# Beethoven's Cat

by

**ELISABET McHUGH**

*Illustrated by*

**ANITA RIGGIO**

A Yearling Book

Published by
Dell Publishing
a division of
Bantam Doubleday Dell Publishing Group, Inc.
666 Fifth Avenue
New York, New York 10103

ISBN: 0-440-40398-7

Reprinted by arrangement with Macmillan Publishing Company, on behalf of Atheneum

Printed in the United States of America

January 1991

10 9 8 7 6 5 4 3 2 1

CWO

*To Marilyn*
*For also being my friend*
—Elisabet McHugh

*For Elissa and Lydia*
—Anita Riggio

# Beethoven's
# Cat

# Chapter
## 〔 1 〕

IT ALL BEGAN ONE EVENING IN NOVEMBER.

As was often the case after dinner, the whole Carter family was assembled in the living room. Everybody was busy doing his or her own thing: Mr. C. was at his desk, working on his dissertation on Beethoven; B. C., the baby, was on the floor on a blanket, contentedly chewing on his rubber alligator; Mrs. C. was, for the third time that week, trying to fix the zipper on Steve's coat. Stevie himself was stretched out on the floor, making weird noises while reading a comic book. His older sister, Cilla, was draped across the couch, surrounded by stacks of teen magazines. She was trying to decide what kind of dress she would get for the high school spring dance, six months from now, should anyone happen to invite her— an unlikely event.

Just for once, everyone was pretty quiet, a phenomenon that in this house occurs about twice a year. I was dozing off myself, curled up in my favorite basket on top of the bookcase.

Like all my baskets—I have two others in strategic places throughout the house—this one was placed as high up off the floor as possible. This keeps me out of immediate danger, should Stevie and Cilla suddenly start a fight. It also allows me to relax and digest my food—which sometimes is quite a task itself—even when Stevie and his buddies are playing around.

For some reason, my friend and colleague Josh (a black-and-white cat of uncertain breed) prefers to live dangerously. He'll go to sleep just about anyplace—on top of the couch, for example, or in a chair, or buried in the sheepskin rug in front of the fireplace. Once he even fell asleep in the clothes dryer. Considering the unpredictability of the members of this household, it's a miracle he's still alive.

But let me get back to that evening. As I mentioned, I was just drifting off to sleep, when all of a sudden Mr. C. began to chuckle. "Hey, Bev," he said. "Look at this. Doesn't it remind you of somebody?" He held up a book that had some kind of picture in it.

Mrs. C. looked up. "Let me see." She got up from her chair and reached for the book. From where I was, peeking over the edge of my basket, all I could see was her back.

Now it was her turn to laugh. "How about that?" she said. "He's not anywhere near as fat, but the likeness is really uncanny." Then, for some reason, she turned around and looked at me. I immediately yawned and adjusted myself to a more comfortable position. I was wondering what was so funny, but since it's considered bad manners to show one's curiosity too openly, I acted as if I couldn't care less what was going on.

Pretty soon, Cilla and Stevie had joined in the general hilarity. The strange thing was that all of them kept on staring first at the book and then at me and then at the book again.

Now Stevie grabbed the book and held it up in front of me. "Look at this, Wiggie," he said. "Here's a picture of you."

Obediently I took a look. The left page showed a blurry photograph of two people I had never seen before. On the opposite page was a peculiar drawing of a man with an oversized head and a small body. I recognized the man, of course. For months now, Mr. C. had been researching the life of the famous German composer Ludwig van Beethoven, and by now there wasn't a thing the whole family didn't know about him. This was old Ludwig, all right, with his bushy gray hair sticking out in all directions.

My eyes moved on to the cat that was portrayed sitting beside him. Slowly, my mouth fell open (Josh told

6

me later that I was gaping like a half-wit), as I stared in horrified fascination at the picture.

With a tingling sensation moving down my spine, I realized that not only did the cat in the drawing show a remarkable resemblance to its master—the same round, puffy cheeks, the same scowl, the same bushy hair—but what was even more incredible was that it was the spitting image of a cat that the whole Carter family knew and loved—me.

# Chapter

# [ 2 ]

". . . AND I'M TELLING YOU THAT I KNOW FOR A FACT
that I'm a direct descendant of Beethoven's cat."

Josh yawned. "Sure," he said disbelievingly. "And
just how do you know that?"

"That's easy. For one thing, his name was Ludwig,
and my name is Ludwig."

Josh blinked. "I thought your name was Wiggie."

"That's a nickname, stupid. When Stevie was little,
he couldn't say Ludwig so he called me Wiggie. Before
I knew it, everybody was calling me Wiggie."

"How come you never told me that before?" Josh
said suspiciously. "After all, I've lived here almost four
years."

"Never mind," I said impatiently. "I'm telling you

8

now." I had no intention of admitting that I had always hated the name Ludwig. But then, of course, I didn't know until now that I was named after such a famous forebear.

"So what? That still doesn't prove anything. There are probably thousands of cats around named Ludwig."

"Who had a *father* named Ludwig?" I raised my eyebrows. "And a *grandfather* named Ludwig? And a *great*-grandfather named Ludwig? And. . . ."

"How can you be so sure that what your mother told you was true? Maybe she made it all up."

I sighed. "Why," I asked patiently, "would she make up a thing like that? It certainly makes perfect sense to me. Families do like to pass names on. Besides, why don't you check up on it yourself? My father was a house cat in the Carter family before Mr. Carter got married. And so was my grandfather. So there."

Josh was still unwilling to admit that I had proved my point. "And what else?" he persisted.

I got up on all fours, arched my back, and yawned. Here it was, almost naptime, and I was still arguing with that stupid cat. "Well," I said. "It's obvious, isn't it? You saw the picture yourself. It's me, from the exact number of whiskers, to the white, heart-shaped patch on the chest, to the gray, long-haired coat with the widely spaced black stripes."

"Lots of cats look the same," Josh said unconvincingly.

"In most cases, yes. In my case, no. *Nobody* looks like me."

Unexpectedly, Josh snickered. "I guess it's true that some people start resembling their pets after they have had them for a long time. Beethoven sure looked a lot like his cat. Or rather," he corrected himself, "the cat looked a lot like Beethoven."

I deliberately refrained from commenting. What had occupied my mind since the previous evening (and had kept me awake most of the night) was a theory that would account for the likeness between Beethoven's cat and myself. It was, in my opinion, the only logical explanation, although so far I had not dared to say it aloud even to myself.

I had slept maybe an hour when Stevie returned home from school. As usual, he slammed the door shut with a bang that made the whole house shake, dumped his backpack on the bench in the hall, and headed for the refrigerator in the kitchen. There he managed to knock down a plastic container with leftovers and upset an entire bowl of apples while digging for the largest one to eat for a snack. The whole thing took about eight seconds, a new record.

You'd think that, with this kind of racket going on all the time, I should be used to it. Well, I'm not. That's why I try to get as much sleep as possible while the kids are in school. If I'm lucky, both of them might go off somewhere after they come home, but more often than not, they bring their friends home with them, which increases the noise level accordingly.

Now I paid a brief visit to the backyard, and after that I looked around for Winston. Being a dog and impervious to the weather, he is likely to be gone for hours, no matter how cold it is. Because of this, I never know where to find him. Having scouted the whole house, I now positioned myself by the pet door to make sure I wouldn't miss him when he returned.

When he finally showed up, he was carrying a bone and had a half-inch layer of snow on his back. Self-preservation made me jump aside just in time, before he started shaking himself. Why anyone in his right mind would want to spend time outdoors in the middle of the winter has always been beyond me. There must be other, less horrible ways of self-torture. I tried once to discuss it with Winston, but my point of view unfortunately was met with total incomprehension.

Winston is a bulldog, which means he has one of those faces that look as if he's run into a wall. Whether this has anything to do with his lack of sensitivity, I really don't know. Actually, we get along fine most of the time, having our daily tug of war with one of Mr. C.'s old socks, an occasional wrestling match, and now and then a friendly game where we push an old rubber ball back and forth between us.

Before Winston moved in with us, which was three years ago when he was still a puppy, we had a German shepherd named Lady. She and I were very close, and it was a sad day when the Carters discovered that she had incurable cancer and had to be put to sleep.

Looking back now, I finally had an explanation for the closeness of our relationship. It was so simple that I should have thought of it before. Lady was of German ancestry, and (as I had discovered last night) so was I. Yes, I thought now, that was another definite indication that I was indeed a descendant of Beethoven's cat.

Figuring that Winston was done shaking himself, I asked now, "Did you see the picture of me?"

He dropped the bone on the floor by his water bowl. "You mean the drawing?"

I nodded.

He drank noisily, splashing water all over the place. "Yep," he said finally, licking his chops. "Sure looks like you, all right."

"I know." I sighed deeply. "It's amazing, isn't it?"

Winston walked over to the box where he keeps his toys. After some poking around, he got hold of his sock. I followed behind him as he headed for the living room.

"Well," he said after dropping the sock, "I don't know whether there's anything amazing about it. It just shows that you're not the only weird-looking cat around."

That really got me. "Now, wait a minute," I said sharply. "Who said anything about looking weird?"

"You did." He lay down. "Isn't that what you've been trying to tell me for years?"

I swallowed a sharp retort. In a way he was right, although what I had been referring to was my extraordinary markings. "I don't remember ever using the word *weird*," I said now.

"Maybe not," he said agreeably. "But I'm telling you, Wiggie boy, that for a cat you sure do look *peculiar*."

"Do you realize that the drawing was of a cat with the same name as I, who lived almost two hundred years ago?"

Winston suddenly looked interested. "You mean his name was Wiggie, too?"

"Of course not," I said, annoyed. "His name was Ludwig, just like my name is Ludwig. Wiggie is a nickname."

Now Winston started laughing, a rumbling laugh that soon developed into hiccups. I looked at him in distaste.

"I'm glad you find it so entertaining," I said stiffly. "In case you didn't know, lots of people have nicknames."

Gradually, he calmed down. "Oh, it's not your nickname that's funny," he gasped. "It's your other name. Ludwig. Imagine calling somebody Ludwig. . . ." Here he went into paroxysms again.

I stared irritably at him. "For your information," I said coldly, "it's an old family name that's been handed down from father to son for generations."

"Really?" Winston hiccuped again. "You'd think

they could have thought of something different. Ludwig. . . . Ha, ha, ha. . . ."

When I left him, he was still in convulsions on the floor.

I went upstairs. Cilla must have brought a friend home from school, because I could hear squeals and giggles from her room. Stevie was probably outside working on his snow fort.

I pushed open the door to the master bedroom. In one daring leap, I reached the top of the dresser where I had my basket. With a little luck, I thought, I'd be able to get some shut-eye before Mr. and Mrs. C. came home from work. If I was able to go to sleep, that is, after Winston's crude behavior.

I was now able to better understand my own sensitive personality. As we had all learned from Mr. C., Ludwig van Beethoven had lived and socialized not only with the aristocracy but also with members of the royal family. So had, probably, his faithful cat Ludwig. I could only imagine the refined company that had surrounded my great ancestor. No wonder, I thought with a shudder, that I was so shocked by Winston's behavior.

Wiggling myself deeper into the blankets in my basket, I tried to picture what Ludwig I, as I shall call him from now on, would have done in a situation like mine. A few moments of consideration gave me the answer. Nothing. Ludwig I would have done nothing. After all, what can you do about bad manners except ignore them?

After yawning a couple of times and scratching my nose, I was finally about to fall asleep, when suddenly, a blood curdling yell pierced the silence of the house. It brought me back to consciousness with a jerk that almost made me fall out of my bed. A moment later, I heard Steve come stomping up the stairs.

I rolled over on my back and stared up at the ceiling. Why, I asked myself in quiet desperation, why does this always happen just when I want to take a nap? Why was I born into a family that has a nine year old who can't even *breathe* quietly? Why me?

Unfortunately, the ceiling (which had a dead fly plastered to it, a relic from last summer) offered no answer.

# *Chapter* ⸢ 3 ⸥

"I'M GOING OVER TO KATHY'S FOR A WHILE," CILLA
announced after dinner. "We have to cram for our history test tomorrow."

"Cram?" Steve crossed his eyes and made one of his
revolting noises. "You mean you have to *cram* to get a
*D*?"

Cilla cut him dead with an icy stare that clearly told
him not to push his luck.

Mrs. C., who was decorating a cake for the church
bake sale, slapped on another portion of frosting, turning
the knife expertly to produce a swirling effect. As usual,
while working she was listening to a language tape. Now
she turned off the tape recorder and turned to her daughter. "Don't stay too late." She added disapprovingly,

"Do you have to wear that horrible lipstick?"

Cilla said untruthfully, "It's the only one I have."

While waiting for their usual exchange of words regarding these matters (in which Mrs. C. always loses out), I licked the last speck of tuna casserole off my whiskers.

"Really? What happened to your other lipsticks?"

Cilla said resentfully, "Mom, you don't understand. Those are all *last* year's colors. If I don't wear what's in, no boy is ever going to pay attention to me."

With a sigh Mrs. C. raised her eyes to the ceiling (presumably in an effort to avoid the sight of Cilla's bluish purple lips). "Don't be late," she repeated finally, returning her attention to the cake. She pushed the button of the cassette recorder, and once more the sound of Finnish reverberated through the kitchen.

I was still trying to decide which sounded worse, Finnish or Danish. I thought now that maybe the former topped the list. After one week of listening to the tape, the staccato sounds of the language still grated unpleasantly on my ears. Admittedly, six months ago when Mrs. C. first tackled Danish, the sound of that had reminded me of a person speaking while bravely trying not to throw up. As time went on, however, I got used to it. Maybe, although it seemed doubtful at the moment, I'd get used to Finnish, too.

Neither language helped with my digestion after dinner. For once, I had to admit that perhaps I had overdone my culinary intake a bit. I felt like a balloon that had been inflated beyond its safety limits. One more puff (or one more bite, rather) and I'd pop.

Besides my usual dinner portion of dry Meow Chow, I had polished off part of a stale ham sandwich found by Mrs. C. in Steve's jeans pocket while sorting the laundry, half of a shriveled-up hot dog, which someone had stuck behind the ketchup bottle in the refrigerator door and then forgotten, and a good-sized serving of leftover tuna casserole.

Usually I have to share extra treats like this with my pals, but, as luck would have it, Josh had—for the past hour—been fast asleep among the cushions on the living room sofa. Winston was absent on one of his frequent outings.

"Come on, Wiggie-pooh," Cilla said now (she's the only one who is allowed to call me that), while bending over to pick me up. "I'll take you with me. You can play with Gwendolyn."

Since my mind was on napping, not playing, the last thing I wanted was to visit the neighbors. Under normal circumstances, I would have escaped before she had a chance to grab me, but in my present bloated condition, my reflexes were somewhat slow. Before I knew it I was firmly wedged in under her arm.

For a moment I was sure I was going to pass out. Having my middle squeezed so soon after eating suddenly transferred the pressure from my stomach up to my head. My eyeballs threatened to fall out, and I was overcome with sudden dizziness. The cold air outside temporarily revived me, but even after Cilla had put me down on the floor in the Bowers's kitchen, I was far from feeling well.

Gwendolyn, a long-haired white Persian, was sitting on the bar counter. After one look at me, she said, "What's the matter, Wiggie?" She sounded concerned. "You don't look at all well. Are you sick?"

For a moment I deliberately ignored her. I was lying on my side, trying to get my breathing back to normal. My heart was pounding like a sledgehammer.

At long last, I said, "I'm trying to digest the four-course dinner I just had. Too much of a strain on my delicate system, I'm afraid." I rolled over on my back and closed my eyes.

"Four-course dinner? Oh, my." Gwendolyn shook her head. "Now, that's what I call fancy living. No wonder you look like a stuffed sausage. Mark my words, one of these days you'll drop dead from a heart attack."

Her statement didn't upset me the least, since she is prone to make similar comments every time I see her. It's just her way to cover up the fact that she really is concerned about my health.

"What's this I hear about you being a descendant of royalty?" Gwendolyn asked.

Feeling better at the thought of my heritage, I made myself comfortable on the rug. "Not royalty," I corrected her. "I'm the descendant of a cat who happened to belong to the great German composer Ludwig van Beethoven. As you may know, Beethoven had many patrons who were members of the aristocracy. After he moved to Vienna, two of his admirers, a prince and a princess, took him in as a member of their household. And"—I paused for a discreet burp—"it was there that Beethoven found Ludwig."

"Ludwig?" Gwendolyn looked bewildered. "You mean he found himself?"

My neighbor may have a heart of gold, but she isn't exactly the brightest cat around. "Not *that* Ludwig," I said patiently. "He found Ludwig the cat, my noble ancestor. Who do you think I'm talking about? Ludwig was only a kitten back then, and Beethoven became so attached to him that he named him after himself."

After pondering this for a moment, Gwendolyn said, "Oh, I see. The kitten was adopted. That was nice of him. Beethoven, I mean."

Unwisely, I rose from my lounging position. The sudden move must have upset my digestion because my stomach protested by making loud gurgling sounds. *"Nice?"* I repeated, more than a little put out. "Beethoven was lucky to *find* Ludwig. It completely changed his life. He—"

"—had to get used to having cat hair all over his furniture. Don't you think I know?" Gwendolyn chuckled. "Then, of course, he had to go to the pet store and buy a litter box, right? And I bet that kitten kept Beethoven awake half the night. . . ."

I closed my eyes. "Never mind, never mind," I said wearily. Why did I, against my better judgment, always get involved in these fruitless conversations? "For your information, they didn't *have* litter boxes back then. We're talking about something that happened almost two hundred years ago, remember?"

Gwendolyn considered this for a moment. Then she said apologetically, "Of course. How stupid of me. I should have figured that out myself. I guess they had pet doors, the kind you have at your house with the rubber flap."

To keep myself from going crazy, I clenched my teeth while staring at a grease spot on the wall. It was not the first time my patience had been pushed to the limit by Gwendolyn. Only a simple soul like her would believe that pet doors with rubber flaps existed during the 1800s.

"Gwenny, you *still* don't understand. Without his cat, Beethoven would never have become famous. Until he found Ludwig I—if I may call him that—Beethoven was merely another talented pianist. It was the cat who inspired him to create some of the greatest music ever written."

For a whole minute Gwendolyn stared back at me with her mouth open. Suddenly her face brightened. "Why, of course," she said. "*Now* I get it. You should have told me earlier that Beethoven played the piano. I knew I'd seen him somewhere. Say," she frowned thoughtfully, "wasn't he on television last week?"

An hour later when Cilla and I were on our way home, I thanked my lucky star I didn't live in the same house as Gwendolyn. If I had to endure conversations like this every day I'd go out of my mind. Thank God for Josh. In spite of his eccentricities, he was normal compared to Gwenny.

Now Cilla scratched my ear and crooned, "Did you and Gwendolyn have a nice visit, Wiggie? I know what good friends you two are. Maybe she could come and stay with us over Thanksgiving while the Bowerses are gone."

The shock made my body go limp, and I almost slid out of Cilla's arms. Gwenny, staying at *our* house?

"Oh, that's right." Cilla paused while brushing the snow off her shoes. "I completely forgot. Kathy told me they are staying home this year. Her grandmother is coming here instead."

Relieved, I felt the blood gradually returning to my head.

Carefully, Cilla put me down on the kitchen floor. Then she said, "I guess you're not hungry after having all those leftovers for dinner . . . but just in case, here's your evening snack."

Two lovely, delectable, plump, juicy sardines reposing on a plate!

"Wiggie, *please!* Stop drooling on my sneakers! And in case you're thirsty, here's a little leftover baby formula that B. C. didn't finish yesterday."

I began eating, completely forgetting how stuffed I had been just an hour or so before.

"My goodness! You're getting to be a real glutton, aren't you," chided Cilla. "Don't forget that you're already overweight. . . . Maybe we should put you on a diet."

Diet? And how many times has your mother told you not to use four-letter words? Hundreds of times, right? Well, diet happens to be one of those words, and if you. . . .

# Chapter
# [ 4 ]

"HEY, WIGGIE! DO YOU WANT TO COME AND WATCH my basketball game this afternoon?" Stevie peeked under the table where Josh and I were positioned, ready to catch any scraps of food that intentionally or unintentionally might fall to the floor.

The thought of spending a whole hour in that smelly gym was not particularly inviting. Last year, Cilla smuggled me in to a junior varsity game, in her duffel bag. By halftime I had almost passed out from the pungent fumes of stinky sneakers and sweaty bodies. In addition, I was practically deaf from all the yelling and screaming and whistling that was going on. When we came home, my nerves were so shattered that it took all the strength and will power I possessed just to swallow my dinner.

Steve continued gleefully: "Since you are the right shape, maybe we can use you for a ball. Just remember to pull in your stomach so you don't get stuck in the net."

Ha, ha. I'm laughing myself to death. I hope the other team uses *you* to sweep the floor with.

Josh tried unsuccessfully to hide a smirk. I decided to ignore it. Sometimes the loyalty of my feline companion is sadly misdirected.

Casually, Cilla let a piece of bacon slide off her fork. Unfortunately, Josh beat me to it by a paw's length. The crunching sound as he devoured it almost brought tears to my eyes. In my opinion, nothing beats the mouth-watering flavor of golden brown, crisp bacon, fried to perfection.

Determined not to miss the next handout, I moved a little closer to Cilla's feet, rubbing myself against her leg to remind her of my presence.

"Pam wants me to go roller-skating with her tonight."

"Again?" Mrs. C., who had B. C. on her lap, tried to hold his bottle with one hand while feeding herself breakfast with the other. "Why this sudden interest in roller-skating? You've gone twice already this week."

Cilla's hand appeared under the table, holding a piece of buttered toast. "It's good exercise," she said vaguely.

I chewed the toast slowly to get the full benefit of

the flavor. It was just the way I like it—soaked with butter.

Stevie said innocently, "You mean hanging around Kenny White's neck and drooling on his shoulder counts as exercise?"

Cilla almost choked on her food. When she had recovered, she said frostily, "I'm sure I don't know what you are talking about."

"Brad and I happened to be at the Skate-a-Rink Wednesday night, but"—Stevie wiped the egg yolk off his plate with a piece of bread—"I guess you were so busy *exercising* that you didn't see us."

"And who is this Kenny?" Mr. C. wanted to know.

Cilla gave her brother a well-aimed kick as she passed his chair. "He's one of the honor students in the sophomore class," she said virtuously. Her face had the expression of someone unjustly accused. "He just happened to be at the rink. . . . Can I go?"

"I guess so." Mrs. C. sighed and handed her the baby. "Could you put his snowsuit on? I have to get ready or I'm going to be late." Mrs. C., who works down at city hall four days a week, drops B. C. off at his sitter on the way to work. Then she picks him up again in the afternoon.

Since everybody was through eating, I turned my attention to supervising the daily operation of easing the youngest member of the Carter family into his suit.

As usual, B. C. was doing his best to delay the departure from home by waving his arms and legs and kicking vigorously every time Cilla tried to squeeze a leg in. After a couple of minutes of this, he unexpectedly rolled over on his stomach (an old ploy but it works every time), forcing Cilla to reverse the suit in order to get it on right. Then, once she had one of his feet halfway in, B. C. grabbed the zipper pull and stuffed it in his mouth while making gagging sounds (his most recent trick). As a result, she had to let go of his leg in order to save him from choking himself.

I watched for another few minutes. In view of the ingenuity B. C. showed at the tender age of six months, there was no telling what great things he might accomplish later on. His stalling tactics while being dressed are impressive, to say the least—but then, of course, he has several months of daily practice behind him.

When I lost interest and went into the living room, Josh was already stretched out in front of the fireplace. Even Winston was getting ready for a morning nap.

"What's the matter?" I asked. "How come you're not outside cultivating frostbite and pneumonia?"

Winston opened one bloodshot eye and glared at me. "It's raining," he rasped. "It has been raining all night. The whole yard is nothing but slush and mud."

"Is *that* all?" I said heartily. "You mean you're letting a minor thing like that keep you from your appointed rounds? Where is your pioneer spirit?"

"*Hrrmpf,*" Winston said, revealing his complete lack

of humor. He closed his eye again. Josh was already asleep, snoring quietly.

With a sigh I retreated to the top of the bookcase. Mr. C. had made a photocopy of the drawing of my famous ancestor and pinned it on the wall above my basket. Since I wasn't quite ready to doze off yet, I made myself comfortable while studying the picture.

Despite the fact that I had spent hours examining every detail of the two characters, I still had an eerie feeling whenever I looked at them. Not only did I have trouble getting used to the incredible likeness between Ludwig I and myself, I also continued to marvel over the uncanny resemblance between him and his master.

As I continued to stare at the picture, I realized that it was beginning to have an almost hypnotic effect on me. I tried to look away, but my eyes were drawn back as if guided by some supernatural force.

What, I wondered now, had caused my ancestor to assume the features of Ludwig van Beethoven? Was it because they had lived together for so long? Or was it because their relationship had been unusually close? Had Beethoven's personality gradually imposed itself on Ludwig I until it affected his physical appearance?

I stared unblinkingly at the drawing until the two faces seemed to blend together into one and I began to doze.

When I awoke a short time later, I saw Mr. C. stretched out in his favorite easy chair, surrounded by books and papers. As usual, he was absorbed in his research. The silence was broken only by an occasional grunt from Mr. C. as he leafed through a pile of papers. Judging by his facial expression, the contents must have been amusing. Now and then, he chuckled to himself.

Josh was curled up on the old wool blanket by the fireplace. "I wonder what's so funny?" he said. "From what I've been able to tell, old Ludwig's life wasn't exactly a barrel of laughs."

As if he had heard him, Mr. C. unexpectedly looked up. He reached for his coffee cup, only to find it empty. With a sigh, he unfolded his lanky figure and headed for the kitchen. In passing, he reached over and scratched my ear. "Did you know, old pal," he said dryly, "that reading about your namesake is like reading about you? You and Beethoven's cat are like two peas in a pod."

I felt an involuntary shiver of excitement at his words. It really was uncanny how my life was becoming more and more linked with that of my ancestor.

My speculations were rudely interrupted by Josh, who emitted a sudden snicker. "Did you hear that, Wiggie? Two peas in a pod. Maybe we should call you Veggie instead. Get it? Veggie." His body shook with suppressed laughter.

Disgusted as I was by his childish behavior, I forced myself to count slowly to ten before responding.

"Really!" My voice was cold. "Personally, I fail to see the humor in the situation. Clearly, Mr. C.'s observation is yet another proof of the relationship between Beethoven's beloved cat and myself. It's obvious that we have more in common than just our physical appearance."

"Oh, yeah?" Josh wiped his eyes. "Such as what?"

Since I had no idea what Mr. C. had been referring to, it took me a moment to come up with a suitable answer. Finally, I said, "Our intellectual pursuits are probably very similar."

While Josh tried to stifle another outburst of hilarity, I continued: "Since Ludwig I lived among scholars and artists, it appears logical to me that his tastes would have been influenced by them. Surrounded as he was by inspiring music and brilliant conversation, he must have acquired a profound love for the cultural arts of his time."

Evidently Josh hadn't listened to a single word. Now he was clinging to the sofa, where he dug his claws into the upholstery. "Isn't that a scream, Wig—Veggie? Two peas in a pod." Overcome by an attack of hiccups, he rolled around on the floor in the most undignified manner. It was a pitiful sight.

An hour later when Mrs. C. returned, Josh had mercifully fallen asleep with a silly grin on his face.

# Chapter
## 【 5 】

MY CURIOSITY ABOUT THE INFORMATION THAT HAD triggered Mr. C.'s remark was not satisfied until a couple of days later.

As was my habit after dinner, I was curled up in my basket on top of the bookcase, trying to digest the substantial meal I had just tucked away. I could see Cilla stretched out on the floor below me. She was deeply engrossed in her homework and from her occasional mutterings I perceived that she was struggling with world history—not one of her favorite subjects.

Yawning discreetly, I wondered idly where Josh might be. As far as I knew, his dinner was still in the kitchen, untouched. Mrs. C. had topped our bowls with pieces of golden crisp chicken skin, and I was toying with the idea of helping myself to his share. The way I looked at it, what Josh didn't know wouldn't hurt him, and who knew when he might show up, anyway? It would be a crime to let the skin go to waste.

I was just about to put my plan into action when Mr. C. suddenly appeared.

"Oh, there you are," he said when he saw Cilla. "Do you have a minute? There's something I'd like you to read."

"Sure, Dad." With evident relief, Cilla pushed her homework aside. "Believe me," she said with an exaggerated groan, "right now I'll read anything instead of world history. And I don't *care* if I flunk the test tomorrow." Sighing deeply, she grabbed a cushion from the sofa and propped it behind her back.

Stevie chose this opportune moment to make his presence known. I hadn't even known he was around, which in itself was a miracle.

"Your teacher would have a heart attack if you passed the test, anyway," he remarked. "The shock would kill her. . . ." He put a hand on his heart and began to stagger around the room. "I don't believe it," he squeaked in a falsetto voice. "For the first time in history, Cilla Carter didn't flunk her test. First time in *world* history," he added meaningfully. "Ha, ha, ha."

Cilla eyed him with distaste. Then she turned around so she wouldn't have to look at him.

" 'Dear Jakob . . .' " she read aloud. Then she frowned. "Who's Jakob?"

Mr. C. adjusted his glasses. "Beethoven's cousin."

"Oh." She started over. " 'Dear Jakob, It pains me to learn of your unsuccessful business venture. As you may recall, I cautioned you very strongly against investing your entire inheritance in a project that from the outset seemed doomed to failure. My own finances are as usual very strained. Even if this were not the case, I would not lend. . . .' " Cilla stopped, puzzled. "Why do you want me to read this?"

Mr. C. said hastily, "Oh, you can skip that part. Just start at the bottom of the first page."

At this point I decided to leave my cozy retreat and venture out to the kitchen. I had just hit the floor when Cilla resumed her reading.

" '. . . as you know, dear cousin, I have always abhorred the presence of animals. In spite of this, I find myself increasingly attached to this cat. He is an endless source of amusement to me while I am working. For one thing, he rubs his face in the most peculiar manner, using both front paws at once, leading one to believe that he is about to blow his nose.' " Cilla looked up. "Hey, Dad," she exclaimed, "isn't that what Wiggie does all the time?"

Mr. C. chuckled. "I know. Read on. There's more."

By now I stood as if rooted to the floor. It was indeed an accurate description of one of my distinctive

33

habits. Obviously, it was this letter that had triggered Mr. C.'s remark about us being "two peas in a pod."

" 'He also,' " Cilla read, " 'prefers to tend to his grooming while lying flat on his back. The apparent inconvenience of trying to reach all areas of his body while in this position is evidently compensated for by the fact that he can, whenever he feels like it, relax and doze off for a couple of minutes before resuming his task. . . .' Gee, Dad, are you sure you didn't write this yourself? It's like reading about Wiggie."

Mr. C. laughed. "It's rather spooky," he admitted. "However, that letter is part of the Beethoven Archives in Bonn, Germany. There is no doubt that it was written by Beethoven."

Now all of them, even Winston, were staring intently at me.

Feeling rather self-conscious by the sudden attention, I decided to join my pal over by the fireplace.

"You know," Winston rumbled, "it is rather amazing."

This was not to be denied. After this, how could anyone possibly question my relationship with Ludwig I? This letter was the final proof.

"Well," I commented modestly, "it only confirms what I already knew."

"Amazing," he repeated. "To imagine that not only was there another cat in existence that *looked* as weird as you, but he also *acted* just as weird."

Stung to the core by this criticism, I was about to make a sharp retort when Stevie suddenly said, "I know what happened. Beethoven's cat rose from the dead and disguised himself as Wiggie."

A cold shiver ran up my spine. Was such a thing really possible? Could it be that I was not only the direct descendant but actually the *reincarnation* of Beethoven's cat?

Cilla came over and scooped me up in her arms. "Is that true, Wiggie-pooh?" she cooed. "Were you someone else's favorite pet before you came here?"

I buried my face in her sweater as another even more frightening possibility presented itself. Since Beethoven had imposed his personality on his cat to such a degree that the cat even began to *look* like him, who was to say that this might not also happen to me?

"Why do you always pick on Wiggie?" she asked resentfully. "He's never done anything to you."

"Maybe he *is* a ghost," Stevie went on dramatically. "A fat, stupid cat during the day, a ghost after midnight." He threw his head back and let out an ear-piercing howl.

Not surprisingly, this quickly brought Mrs. C. on the scene. "What on earth . . . ?" she began. Then, spotting Steve, she sighed in exasperation. "I'm trying to get the baby to go to sleep."

"Sorry, Mom."

Winston, who had been watching Stevie from under

half-closed eyelids, said unexpectedly, "Can you imagine having more than one like him in the family?"

I extracted myself from Cilla's arms. "Maybe he'll outgrow it," I said.

Now Steve was trying to balance a book on his nose. He weaved dangerously back and forth, bumping into various pieces of furniture in the process. As he was working himself closer to where we were, I suddenly remembered the chicken skin. Grateful for an excuse to leave, I fled to the kitchen.

# Chapter

## 【 6 】

SATURDAY MORNING I WAS THE FIRST ONE UP AS usual. The rest of the family likes to sleep in on weekends, and last night they had been to a concert that ended rather late. Josh and Winston are late risers no matter what day of the week it is, so I didn't expect them to show up for a while, either.

The drawback with weekends is that I have to wait for my breakfast until someone else gets up. Driven by pangs of hunger, I now began a methodical search for something to placate my rumbling stomach.

Some days there are all kinds of tidbits lying around. Mr. C., for example, likes to munch on cheese and hardboiled eggs between meals. Occasionally, some of it is left on his desk or by his favorite chair. Mrs. C. nibbles on raw vegetables. Those may be good for her but personally I'd rather starve than eat things like carrots or cauliflower.

Stevie, on the other hand, has excellent taste when it comes to food, although his table manners are disgusting, and liberally scatters potato chips, cheese crackers, pieces of cupcakes, and other goodies all over the place. Cilla, who has a sweet tooth, either pigs out on chocolate-chip cookies or else, when she has trouble getting into her jeans, goes on a yogurt binge. Either way, she is liable to leave some of it around for me.

In spite of all this, there are unfortunately mornings when there isn't as much as a crumb to be found.

Having checked the floors, first in the living room and then the kitchen, without finding more than half a potato chip, I now made a leap up onto the counter by the sink. The sight of what was there was so startling that I instinctively took a step back, almost falling over the edge again. Right under my nose was a barely touched, scrumptious cheesecake, topped with an inch-thick layer of sour cream and garnished with sliced strawberries.

What, I wondered, had I done to deserve such a feast on a dull, dreary morning like this? And who had forgotten to put the cake away last night?

With my eyes glued to the glorious vision in front of me, I adjusted myself to a more comfortable position before digging in.

Almost half an hour later, unable to swallow another

bite, I descended from the counter somewhat less gracefully than normal. This was, of course, due to the fact that I was so stuffed I could hardly move. It had been a long time since I'd gorged myself like this. As I proceeded across the kitchen floor, for some reason I was forced to walk with my legs spread wider apart than usual. My stomach (slightly swollen, I must admit) seemed to be in the way.

Slightly out of breath, I squeezed myself through the pet door. Not for the first time I wished the Carters would install one with a larger opening. After all, the present door had been there since I was a kitten and was not quite suitable for a fully grown cat with a well-proportioned figure like mine. It never ceases to surprise me how easily Winston slips through, in spite of his rather prominent potbelly.

When I came back inside, Josh was sitting in front of the refrigerator, yawning.

"Hi, there," he said when he saw me. "And how are you today, Wiggie?"

I frowned. "In deference to my noble heritage," I said stiffly, "I would, from now on, like to be known as Ludwig."

Josh stared at me for a second. "Ludwig, huh?" He paused. "Sure, if that's what you want." He seemed about to add something, but instead he looked around the kitchen. "No breakfast yet? I knew it. I should have stayed in bed."

I burped discreetly. My tummy was now making funny noises. I wondered if maybe I had eaten a little too quickly, not giving my body enough time to digest the food.

"Today is your lucky day," I said now, waving a paw in the direction of the cheesecake. "I saved the rest for you. Be my guest."

In a flash, Josh was up on the counter. His eyes grew round at the sight of the cake. "Wow!" he exclaimed, rubbing his paws together. "Cheesecake! My favorite!"

Feeling slightly nauseated, I decided to retreat to the living room. I couldn't understand the reason for the unsettled feeling in my stomach. Had the sour cream topping gone bad overnight? Or was it perhaps the cheese filling?

I looked up at my basket on top of the bookcase. For some reason, the distance from the floor seemed greater than usual. A wave of dizziness swept over me, and I closed my eyes while holding onto my poor tummy.

After emitting a rather loud belch, I felt a bit better. I looked up toward the bookcase again. Both Beethoven and Ludwig seemed to scowl disapprovingly at my uncivilized manners. Well, I thought, you wouldn't feel too chipper, either, if you had eaten almost half of a double-layered cheesecake for breakfast.

Suddenly I couldn't wait to curl up in my soft, comfortable bed. Maybe a short nap would restore my energy and bring me back to normal. Comforted by this thought,

I took aim and jumped up on the bookcase.

For once I must have miscalculated, because instead of landing with all four feet in my usual spot beside the basket, I barely reached the edge of the top shelf with my front paws. In my frantic attempts to secure a foothold, I finally managed to grab the side of my basket. Then I toppled backward and hit the floor with a crash, bringing the basket down with me.

The last thing I remembered was the feeling of being smothered by something that was soft and fuzzy. Then everything went black.

## Chapter

## [ 7 ]

AS SOON AS I OPENED MY EYES, I WAS SEIZED BY panic. Everything was still in total darkness. It was a moment before I realized I was buried underneath the basket. I breathed a sigh of relief. The soft, fuzzy thing over my face was my favorite blue blanket.

I wiggled my body trying to get out, but I was securely pinned to the floor by the combined weight of the basket, the mattress, and the blanket.

Suddenly I heard Mrs. C. calling. Due to my trapped position, the sound of her voice was rather muffled.

"Is that you, Stevie? What on *earth* is going on down there? Did you break something?"

Sorry, Mrs. C., I thought, this time it is just your favorite cat breaking his neck. Plus a rib or two. Maybe a minor concussion. A few bruises. Nothing very important.

"Did you hear me?"

Why couldn't she hurry up and come down instead? What if I suffocated from lack of air before she found me? Being buried alive had never been on my list of Fun Things to Do on a Saturday Morning.

To my relief, I finally heard her coming down the stairs. I would have meowed to get her attention, but unfortunately my mouth was full of woolly fibers from my blanket. I tried to spit them out. What was taking her so long, anyway?

"Oh, no-o!"

In spite of the protection offered by my padding, Mrs. C.'s high-pitched cry startled me.

"My *beautiful* cheesecake!" Another loud wail. "Josh, how *could* you!"

Yeah, how could you! Shame on you, Josh, eating Mrs. C.'s delicious cheesecake. Don't you know you're not supposed to touch food that happens to be left out on the counter? Naughty, naughty cat!

"*Shame* on you, Josh! And just look at the *mess* you made!"

On second thought, it was kind of cosy under the old basket. With a little luck, I should be able to stay undetected until lunchtime.

Now I could hear someone else walking into the kitchen.

44

"Mom!" That was Cilla. "What's going on? And what's the matter with Josh? Look, he's got white stuff smeared all over his face."

"He ate my cheesecake, that's what's going on." Mrs. C.'s voice was shaking. "The whole cake. There's hardly anything left. And when I think of all the effort I. . . ."

"Didn't you put it away last night?"

"Your father was supposed to do it. How come I can't trust anybody but myself in this house? It took me *hours* to make that cake. . . ."

"Hey, Mom!" Stevie made a noisy arrival as usual. That kid manages to trip over something even when there is nothing around to trip over except an empty floor. "Could I have a piece of cake for breakfast?"

I didn't hear what response that got him, because right then I heard Josh whispering, "Wiggie?"

"Ludwig," I mumbled automatically.

"Wiggie, are you there?"

I rocked the basket to show him I was there.

"That was a great cake."

Now I heard footsteps approaching.

"Oh, there you are, Josh. Come on, now, don't try to sneak away." Cilla's voice was stern. "Let me clean you off a bit. My goodness, you really must have stuffed yourself. . . . Your tummy is like a balloon. . . . Now, stop scratching and be a good boy."

For a moment I felt sorry for my pal. Cilla was

probably wiping him with a wet washcloth. "I just don't understand how you could have eaten all that cake. I only had one measly slice last night and, believe me, I was full."

I lay immobile, hoping that Cilla would leave without discovering where I was. Time enough to be rescued later on when everybody had calmed down.

"Well," Cilla continued briskly, "I guess you won't be needing any breakfast today. Or dinner, for that matter. I just hope you don't get sick. Will you stop wiggling? I'll let you down again in a second. . . . I'm almost done."

Now I had fuzzy things in my nose, too. Bravely, I fought an urge to sneeze. Wasn't she done yet? If I could just control myself until she left. . . .

"There you are, all nice and clean again."

My nose was driving me crazy, but at last I heard footsteps moving away. . . .

"Oops!" She stopped. "What happened here? Who knocked this down? Have you guys been fighting again?"

Suddenly, my protective cover was whisked away. "Oh, Wiggie-pooh!"

I blinked a couple of times to adjust my eyes to the light.

"Oh, you poor baby." She picked me up and hugged me tightly. I felt a twinge of pain in my back. Quite possibly my spine was broken.

46

"What happened, sweetie? How long have you been stuck under there?" She rubbed my ears while making comforting sounds. "And why didn't you say something, Wiggie-baby? You know Cilla would have been right there to help you."

Josh, who was sitting on the floor cleaning his paws, muttered morosely, "How could you? You were too busy sloshing water all over me."

I turned my head. "You should be grateful," I pointed out. "She just wanted to help."

Now Cilla carried me into the kitchen. Mrs. C. was over by the stove making scrambled eggs and sausage, while Stevie was popping bread into the toaster.

"Guess what, Mom?" Cilla said indignantly. "Somebody knocked down Wiggie's basket on the floor, and he was trapped under it and couldn't get out."

Stevie made one of his disgusting sounds. "Serves him right. Besides, he probably knocked it down himself."

I bared my teeth at him.

Cilla frowned at her brother, while cuddling me protectively. "He could have gotten killed, you know." She kissed my nose.

"Oh, yeah?" Stevie had buttered four slices of toast. Now he stacked them on top of each other and started eating. "He looks all right to me."

Immediately, I let out a cry of distress while slumping against Cilla's shoulder. She said worriedly, "Where is it hurting, baby?" Then, addressing Steve, she added reproachfully, "For your information, Wiggie has been through a *very* traumatic experience."

To emphasize my pitiful condition, I closed my eyes and moaned again. Cilla rubbed my chin. "I bet you were trapped under that basket for hours, weren't you?"

Mrs. C., who still looked upset, gave the skillet a vigorous shake. "Josh was probably chasing him," she said in a tight voice. "Wanted all the cheesecake to himself, no doubt."

Did you hear that, Josh, old boy? Shame on you! It's not nice to be greedy. I guess I was lucky to have had a few bites myself before you showed up.

Cilla carefully put me down on the table while she filled my food bowl to the rim with Meow Chow. In order to maintain my injured-cat image, I stretched out on my side while assuming an expression of suffering.

Steve stared unblinkingly at me for a moment before forcing the remainder of the toast into his mouth. His eyes bulged from the effort. If it had been Cilla, she would have given me a piece first.

Now Cilla took a strip of bacon and crumbled it on top of the cat food. I started drooling at the sight. After that, she filled another bowl with milk.

While chomping away on my breakfast, I gave Josh a fleeting thought of pity. No breakfast and no dinner. Well, Josh, old pal, that's what happens when you get caught doing something you shouldn't be doing.

As soon as I had licked both of my bowls clean, Cilla picked me up and tucked me under her arm. "Wiggie and I are going back to bed for a while," she announced. She was holding a plate with her own breakfast in one hand, while carrying a glass of milk in the other. I could feel my face turn blue from the pressure of her arm, but I figured I'd probably survive the trip upstairs.

A moment later I was all snuggled up under the comforter in Cilla's bed. As far as Saturday mornings went, this had decidedly been one of the better ones.

As my eyelids grew heavy, I wondered about the possibility of Mrs. C.'s baking another cheesecake today. Not that I expected it to be left out again, of course, but then, you never knew. . . .

# Chapter

# [ 8 ]

"GREETINGS, WIG . . . I MEAN LUDWIG. STILL IN BED, I see." That was Josh. It was an afternoon several days later. Now it was almost time for Mrs. C. to return from work.

"Not *still* in bed," I corrected him. "I'm in bed again. Not that it makes any difference, of course. I haven't slept a wink since you left. Where have you been?"

"Oh," Josh said vaguely. "Here and there."

Under normal circumstances, an answer like that would not have satisfied me. Today, I was too exhausted to tackle the subject. I suspected Josh of having a new romance going on. His last girl friend, whose name I had never been able to remember, had moved away some weeks ago, and consequently I had expected this to happen for some time.

"Oh, by the way"—it was almost too much of an effort for me even to speak—"I ate your lunch a little while ago. It seemed a shame to leave it around to spoil. I hope you don't mind."

"Not at all." Josh licked his chops. "I had a lunch date, anyway. And if you want to know what I ate—how does a whole can of creamed chicken with liver sound to you? It happens to be the latest recipe from Dainty cat foods. Absolutely dee-licious."

Understandably, my lack of response struck Josh as being highly unusual. Then, unconsciously, my face puckered up into a scowl and I pulled at my own hair with my paws. As soon as I became aware of what I was

doing (it was not the first time this had happened during the last few days), I closed my eyes and tried to relax.

"You really do have a problem, don't you." There was genuine concern in his voice. "Why don't you let Uncle Josh help you?"

"I wish I could." With a feeble attempt at joking, I added, "Maybe I should write to Dear Abby."

"No, seriously," Josh continued earnestly. "You know, I think part of your problem is that you spend too much time by yourself, brooding. You need to get out more. Why don't you go over and visit Gwendolyn for a while?"

I shuddered. "No, thanks."

"Then at least let me introduce you to our new neighbors down the street. A family named Johnson. They have two cats, Snowy and Susie. Snowy is a gray tabby and Susie a Siamese."

Judging by the tone of his voice, Susie must be his latest conquest. "I never thought the day would come when you'd fall for a Siamese," I said dryly.

Josh sighed deeply. "Susie is different," he said dreamily. "There is something about the way she walks. . . . The moment I first laid eyes on her I knew she was the girl I had been looking for all my life."

I refrained from commenting on this. Frankly, I had lost track of the number of times Josh had made that exact same statement. Instead I said, "I'm afraid I wouldn't be very good company right now. I've got too many things on my mind."

I crawled out of my basket and jumped down on the floor. There I stretched and yawned a couple of times.

"Good grief!" Josh stared at me. "You look terrible." He looked up at the picture on the wall, then back at me.

"I know, I know." I stifled another yawn. "There's no need to rub it in."

Josh continued unheeding: "You're beginning to look more and more like Ludwig in the picture. Just wait until Mrs. C. sees you. She'll have a fit."

"So what?" I tried to sound nonchalant, even though I knew all too well that she wanted her beloved cats to be well groomed. "I'm too down in the dumps to bother with my looks. To tell you the truth, I don't think I'll ever care about my appearance again."

"You're kidding." Josh frowned. "You mean you *like* looking like a dust mop?"

I was too tired to go into explanations about why my coat was such a mess. Josh probably wouldn't believe me if I told him that half the time I wasn't even aware that I was tugging and twisting my hair until it was standing on end.

"I happen to like it this way," I said stubbornly. "But then, of course," I added meaningfully, "I don't have a girl friend to impress."

"Maybe you should have Mrs. C. take you to the vet," he suggested now. "It's amazing what a couple of shots will do to perk you up."

Since this wasn't even worthy of an answer, I kept

my silence and made my way toward the pet door. As I squeezed through, I felt something wet on my face. It was raining again.

Unfortunately, Josh's prediction came true. As soon as she had changed B. C.'s diaper and warmed his bottle, Mrs. C. dug the comb and brush out of the kitchen drawer, and followed me upstairs.

"Come on, Wiggie," she said coaxingly. "I'll give you a nice brushing. I don't know how you manage to make such a mess of yourself, but don't worry, we'll soon get you back to normal again. You're looking as disheveled as Beethoven himself."

Carefully, I backed out of her reach. The last thing I wanted right now was to be combed.

"Come on, baby. It will only take a minute."

Why me? Couldn't she get Josh instead?

"What's the matter, Wiggie?" She sounded worried. "Why are you hiding under the dresser?"

Too late I realized I hadn't picked a very good hiding place. It was awfully cramped. They certainly don't make dressers the way they used to.

"It's no use, Wiggie. Come on, now. If you don't I'll have to drag you out."

Mrs. C. almost pulled my legs out of their sockets. Somehow I had gotten stuck, although I couldn't understand why. The last time I was under this particular dresser, there had been plenty of room.

"Want me to do anything, Mom?" That was Cilla.

"Just help me to lift the dresser, will you? I don't know what's gotten into Wiggie. He always loves to be groomed but today for some reason he won't cooperate."

I wished they wouldn't make such a big deal out of it. I was not in the mood, that was all.

"Here he is, Mom. I'll hold him for you."

Two against one. That wasn't fair.

Of course, it was pretty comfy there in Cilla's lap, especially while she rubbed my nose and scratched my ears. It relaxed my muscles and made me drowsy. Not that I wasn't pretty tired already. Last night I had only slept nine hours and today I had hardly closed my eyes all day.

I knew it wasn't very polite to yawn in people's faces, but, like I said, lying on my back like this tended to make me feel drowsy. Who knew, I might even fall asl—

*Chapter*

{ 9 }

"WOULD SOMEBODY PLEASE CARRY IN THE GROCER-ies?" Mrs. C. stumbled into the living room and collapsed in her favorite chair. She looked beat.

"What happened?" asked her husband. "You look like you've been through World War II."

"Believe me, it was worse than that." Tiredly, Mrs. C. unzipped her coat and kicked off her boots. "I was over in the produce section at the supermarket when they announced that six twenty-four-pound turkeys would be sold at half the regular price on a first-come, first-served basis. You should have been there! Everybody went crazy—including me."

"Did you get one?" Steve asked interestedly.

"Did I get one?" Mrs. C. sounded hurt. "Don't you

have any faith in your own mother? Of course, I did. In fact, I got two. Now we don't have to buy one for Christmas."

B. C., who was lying on a blanket in his playpen, responded with loud and enthusiastic gurgles. Then he started pounding on the floor with his rattle.

"Thank you, sweetie," Mrs. C. said gratefully. "I'm glad somebody appreciates my efforts to save money. Take my advice and don't be in such a hurry to grow up. It's a tough world out there."

The mention of turkey (one of my favorite foods) had made me postpone my intended after-dinner snooze. Thanksgiving was almost here, and as far as I was concerned it couldn't come soon enough. It was Mrs. C.'s habit to always purchase the biggest turkey she could find, which resulted in enough leftovers to last us until Christmas. The leftovers from the Christmas turkey usually lasted even longer, because by then everybody would be tired of eating the same old thing and Mrs. C. would be hard pressed to think of new ways to disguise it.

"Speaking about food," her husband said now. Already his mind was back on his research papers. "I found another reference about Beethoven's affection for his cat. Listen to this: 'Although Beethoven was rude to his benefactors and despised his colleagues, he showed an unfailing consideration toward his cat. The servants had orders to provide freshly caught fish for the cat twice a day. On those occasions when they failed to do this, Beethoven invariably flew into a rage, frequently attacking the servants physically. On one occasion, he even broke the arm of one of the scullery maids.' "

"I wish you wouldn't tell me these things." Mrs. C.'s face registered disapproval. "I still don't understand why you couldn't have picked a more sympathetic character for your dissertation. Obviously, Beethoven was nothing but a selfish, overbearing monster. He doesn't deserve to be. . . ."

"The man was a genius," her husband reminded her somewhat pompously.

Mrs. C. picked up her coat. "Only when it came to music."

"Maybe so," Mr. C. said placatingly, "but you also have to remember that at this point in Beethoven's life his deafness was becoming increasingly worse. Imagine how frustrating that must have been for someone like him. No wonder he was short tempered."

"That's still no excuse for his behavior," Mrs. C. persisted. "Imagine breaking somebody's arm just because she didn't remember to get fish for his cat! You call that *normal*?"

"They could have given the cat something else to eat," Steve pointed out. "Or let him go and find his own food. I bet they had plenty of mice and rats and things like that back then . . . maybe even bats."

Mr. C. gave him a disapproving glance over his

reading glasses. "According to this book, the cat only ate fish. He didn't like anything else."

Winston, who was stretched out by the playpen, said to me. "Did you hear that? You'd think he'd get tired of eating the same thing all the time."

I opened my eyes and yawned. "Look who's talking?" I said. "Don't you eat Doggie Chow-chow every day?"

"What if I do? At least I eat a variety of flavors. This week, for example, it's beef-and-liver. Last week it was chicken-tuna and the week before that it was. . . ."

Interrupting him, I said reasonably, "And maybe Ludwig I ate a different kind of fish every day."

*"Hrmmm."* Winston scratched his ear. "As far as I'm concerned, fish is fish. They are all the same."

I was just going to repudiate his statement when I heard Mr. C. mention my name.

". . . acting strange lately?"

Mrs. C. bent over the playpen and picked up the baby, who had started crying. She checked to see if he needed to be changed. "What do you mean?" she asked now, while motioning to Cilla to go and get a dry diaper.

"Well, he seems to spend all his time just lying around. He doesn't chase Josh around anymore. And I haven't seen him play with Winston since I don't know when."

Mrs. C. handed the wet diaper to Steve and asked him to take it to the bathroom. Steve obeyed reluctantly, holding the smelly diaper at arm's length and making retching sounds as he left.

Happy again, B. C. grasped one of his feet and started chewing on his toes. Mrs. C. made sure he was securely wedged in between the cushions on the couch before she turned to look at me. I stared back at her, listlessly. If only they knew. Not for the first time I wished there was some way we could really communicate. But even so, I thought pessimistically, there was probably nothing they could do to help me.

"Now that you mention it," Mrs. C. said thoughtfully, turning her attention back to B. C., "Wiggie really hasn't been himself. Did you know that the other day when I tried to give him a brushing he actually hid under the dresser? He really looked like a mess, too. I wonder if he's coming down with something. Maybe we should take him to the vet for a checkup."

The vet? The hairs rose on my back. Practically every time I visited the vet clinic I either got a shot of some kind or else I got stitched up. Sometimes it was both. It's not exactly what I'd call my favorite place.

Suddenly Josh came sauntering in. He'd been gone most of the afternoon, no doubt spending it in the company of his girl friend. Now he sat down and started cleaning the mud off his paws. "Did I just hear someone mention the vet?" he said. "I thought we were all up-to-date with our shots."

Ignoring him, I addressed Winston: "How about a

tug-of-war, old pal? It's been a long time." There was nothing I felt less like doing than to pull that dirty sock back and forth, but obviously a desperate situation required desperate measures.

"Tug-of-war? We-e-ell. . . ." Winston was clearly enjoying himself. "I'm not sure I feel like it right now. But then again"—he licked his chops and tried to look innocent—"I might get in the mood if I knew there was something in it for me."

I was deeply shocked. "But that's blackmail!"

"You mean you think it's dishonest?"

"Of course, it's dishonest."

"Really?" Winston looked smug. "But *you* want to pretend to be your old normal self—which you are not—by playing a game you really don't want to play. Isn't that just as dishonest?"

I glared at him. "That," I said haughtily, "is simple self-preservation."

A few minutes later, we (or at least Winston) were enthusiastically pulling at the sock, with Stevie acting as self-appointed referee. He climbed up on the coffee table and rolled up a magazine to use as a megaphone.

"Ladies and gentlemen," he announced importantly, "here we have the current champion, Winston 'Bulldog' Carter, trying to defend his title against the fe-rocious Ludwig Carter, also known as Wiggie the Wildcat.

"At the moment, Bulldog has the situation in hand,

61

or rather"—Stevie gave a fake laugh—"the sock in mouth, if you see what I mean. Wildcat is, however, giving him a tough time. Despite being grossly over-weight"—here I almost lost my grip on the sock when I bared my teeth and hissed at Steve—"he is certainly putting up a good fight. Is there a chance that Wildcat might take the title? Well, ladies and gentlemen, that is the big question tonight here at Madison Square Garden."

"Give up?" Winston asked, through clenched teeth.

"Okay." Completely out of breath, I flopped down on the floor. I figured we probably had played long enough, anyway.

Stevie jumped down from the table. "And the winner is. . . ." He held Winston's paw up in the air. "The winner is . . . Bulldog Carter, still undefeated." He held a pretend mike in front of Winston's nose. "And how does it feel to have won again, Bulldog? Pretty good, huh?"

Winston took the opportunity to generously slobber all over Stevie's hand.

"*Yukk.*" Stevie made a face and wiped his hand on his jeans.

"Serves you right." Cilla smiled sweetly at him. "You and your stupid pretend games. Even B. C. thinks you're childish. Don't you, baby?" She tickled B. C.'s tummy until he started laughing. "Hear that?"

"Well, I guess Wiggie is all right, after all," said her mother. I breathed a sigh of relief. "Maybe the weather has been getting to him, too. Nothing but snow and slush and more snow. Remember last year when we went on a picnic down by the river the day after Thanksgiving? It was so sunny and warm we didn't even wear our coats."

With the threat of the vet clinic off my back, I soon perked up. After a while I padded into the kitchen to see what there was for a snack. Josh followed right behind.

I stared at my bowl in dismay. "Meatballs!"

"That's right." Josh was already packing it in. "Yummy, aren't they?"

"But meatballs!" I said again. "I was hoping for a couple of sardines. Or maybe herring in sour-cream sauce."

Josh's mouth fell open. He closed it again just in the nick of time to keep his food from falling out. Then he swallowed and said, "I don't believe I'm hearing right. What's gotten into you all of a sudden, Wig . . . Ludwig? First time I've ever heard you complain about the food. I mean, everybody knows you'll eat anything."

I was too upset to challenge this unfair statement. Also, for some reason my head had started aching. "I happen to have a craving for fish tonight," I said peevishly. "What's wrong with that? That's what I like best. Fish!"

"Oh, for pete's sake." Josh sounded disgusted.

"Here." I pushed the bowl over to him. "You eat it."

When I left the kitchen, Josh was still staring after

me. "You'd better not come and ask for it later on," he warned.

"Don't worry," I said reassuringly. "I won't."

My stomach was making little hungry noises as I curled up in my basket. I sniffled a couple of times, feeling acutely sorry for myself. It was a long time until breakfast.

Besides, I thought dejectedly, what were the chances of getting fish for breakfast, anyway? Probably nil. Maybe I should have eaten the meatballs, after all. But the mental picture of the brown juicy lumps of meat glistening with gravy only managed to make me feel nauseated.

I closed my eyes and tried to keep my mind on neutral subjects, but invariably my thoughts reverted to food. When, at long last, I fell asleep I had a nightmare. I dreamed I was paddling around in a gigantic fish tank trying to catch one of the hundreds of fishes swimming around me. Standing over the tank was Beethoven himself, gesticulating wildly, urging me to go after the fish. Whenever I slowed down he became more agitated. I tried desperately to catch at least one, but whenever a fish was within my reach it somehow managed to slip away, leaving me with empty paws and an even emptier stomach.

# Chapter

## { 10 }

BREAKFAST CONSISTED OF MEOW CHOW AND A PIECE of stale bran muffin. Bleary-eyed from lack of sleep, I stared apathetically at the food. I was hungry, yet I didn't feel like eating.

Since Josh wasn't around, I turned to Winston. "I think I'll go back to bed," I said. "Wake me up after lunch, will you?"

Winston looked at me. For some reason his eyes always seemed to be bulging more in the morning. "What about your breakfast?" he asked now. "You haven't even touched it."

"I know. You can have it if you want to. I was hoping we'd have fish."

"Fish?" He stared blankly at me. "Whatever gave

you that idea? When did we ever have fish for breakfast?"

"Never mind," I mumbled. "It was just a thought."

"If you want my opinion," Winston continued. "you're taking this 'I'm-a-descendant-of-Beethoven's-cat' business a little too far. Just because that cat only ate fish, that doesn't mean that you have to do the same."

"You don't understand," I said tiredly. "I can't help myself. They are trying to take over my life."

"They?"

"Beethoven and Ludwig I."

Winston scratched his head in confusion. "But they are dead."

I laughed bitterly. "In that case, why can't I get them out of my mind? Why do I think of them every moment I'm awake? And why is it that whenever I go to sleep, they are both in my dreams? They never leave me alone."

"If you'll excuse me for saying so," Winston said, "the whole thing seems fishy—ha, ha, get it, Wiggie?—it seems fishy to me. When I was a puppy I had a nightmare once. My mother told me it was caused by indigestion. She said I gobbled down my food too fast. Maybe that's your problem, too."

I stared dully at the floor. "He's trying to make me do something."

"Who is?"

"Beethoven."

"Uh . . . what does he want you to do?"

66

"How do I know?" I sighed. "He only speaks German, which I don't understand."

Winston pondered this for a moment. Then his face lit up. "I know. Tell him that whatever it is he wants you to do, you won't do it."

"Do what?" Josh suddenly appeared, fresh in from the cold.

"Beethoven is trying to get Wig . . . eh . . . Ludwig to do something," Winston explained.

"Is that so?" Josh sat down and started to groom himself. "Personally, I think this reincarnation theory is a bit too farfetched. I mean, it doesn't even make sense. Why would a world-famous German composer want to come back in the form of a plain, ordinary American house cat?"

"And why not?" I said hotly. "After all, I'm a descendant of his cat. It said in Mr. C.'s book that Beethoven was overcome by grief when Ludwig I died. He even composed a minuet to honor his memory."

Winston, who had been staring into space, said suddenly, "That's it."

"That's what?"

"What Beethoven is trying to tell you." Winston was trembling with excitement. "He wants you to write down a composition for him."

After a moment, I said slowly, "You could be right, you know. Maybe . . . maybe he had this tune in his head, all ready to go. And then—before he had a chance to get it down in writing—he died."

Josh said skeptically, "Assuming that you are right—which I don't believe for a moment—how are you going to handle that? You don't know how to write music."

I slumped down on the floor, feeling more depressed than ever. "I guess you're right," I said dully. "If that's what he wants, I still can't do it." And, I thought, if it was something else . . . but then I might never find out what it was Beethoven wanted me to do.

Feeling more dead than alive, I dragged myself out of the kitchen. Too weak to do any strenuous exertions, such as jumping up on a bookcase, I decided to retire to my basket on Mr. C.'s desk in the den. In a moment I was asleep.


When I opened my eyes, hours later, Gwendolyn's homely face was only an inch away from mine. She was staring intently at me. Startled by the sight, I hurriedly shut my eyes again. Where on earth had *she* come from?

Worriedly, I racked my brains. Had I perhaps gone to sleep at her place? No—not as far as I could remember. But then, why was I seeing Gwendolyn? I pondered this question for a moment before coming to the conclusion that I hadn't really seen her. I had only imagined seeing her.

Yes, I decided, that was the only logical explanation. I was dreaming. Not that I knew why I'd be dreaming about Gwendolyn, of course, but stranger things had happened.

I waited awhile before slowly cracking one eye open. Yes, Gwendolyn's face was still there. This time I shut my eyes really tight, while trying to figure out what the dream was all about.

Suddenly a terrible thought struck me: What if I was dead?

Gradually my blood turned to ice. Was it possible that I had passed away in my sleep from lack of food? But, I reasoned, if I was dead, then Gwendolyn must be dead, too.

"Wiggie?" My reflections were unexpectedly interrupted by a soft whisper.

Was this the way they talked in heaven? Or . . . I felt a sudden stab of alarm. The idea was ridiculous, of course, but was it possible that I was not in heaven, but some other place . . . ?

"Wiggie, can you hear me?" There was the whispering voice again.

Still with my eyes tightly shut, I whispered back, "Yes, I can hear you."

"Are you all right?"

"Yes," I whispered. "I'm fine."

"We have been worried about you."

"We?"

"Winston and I."

Good grief! I was so shocked I almost forgot to keep my eyes shut. Was Winston here, too?

"What happened to him?" I asked, still in a whisper.

69

"What happened to whom?"

"Winston."

Then I heard Winston's rumbling voice. "What in the world is he talking about?"

"I don't know." Gwendolyn sounded worried. "Maybe he's dreaming."

Winston grunted. "I know what it is. All that rich food has finally caught up with him. His brain is so embedded in fat that it isn't getting enough oxygen. Sooner or later it was bound to happen."

Outraged by this insulting statement, I sat up with a jerk, tipping over my basket in the process. Gwendolyn, who was sitting right by me, backed off rather hastily and almost fell off the desk.

After untangling myself from the basket, I glared angrily at Winston. "Fatty brain, huh?" I exclaimed indignantly. "And since when are you such an authority on brains? Yours certainly isn't anything to brag about."

"Sorry, old man," Winston replied apologetically. "I was just trying to come up with an explanation for your lack of appetite, that's all. Can't remember ever seeing you skip a meal before. Tucking away extra goodies is more your style, ha, ha, ha." He chuckled. "Say," he added after a moment, "have you ever thought of joining Weight Watchers?"

Now Gwendolyn spoke up. "Will you guys please stop your quibbling?" she said sternly. "I'm sure Wiggie has a perfectly logical reason for not eating his breakfast.

"And if you're wondering why I'm here, Wiggie," she continued, "Winston asked me to come over because he was worried about you. First you skipped breakfast and then you slept all day as if you were dead."

I shuddered inwardly at her choice of words. Personally, I was relieved to know I was still counted among the living.

"You don't happen to have any fish at your house, do you?" I asked.

Winston gave a loud snort.

"Well," Gwendolyn said cautiously. "We have three."

"Really?" I licked my chops. Already I could smell the delicate aroma. . . . My spirits rose considerably. "What kind?"

She frowned. "I'm not sure. Peter and Paul are kind of bluish in color. Mary is brown and a little smaller."

"Peter and Paul?" I said stupidly.

For some reason Winston was rolling around on the floor, laughing his head off.

". . . and Mary. Kathy has the aquarium in her room. You must have seen them when you were there."

Aquarium?

"Why are you asking, anyway?"

"Yeah, Wig . . . Ludwig," Winston guffawed. "Why are you asking? You're not thinking of paying them a little friendly visit, are you? Or are you planning on having them over for lunch?"

I gave him a murderous glare.

"Just asking," I muttered to Gwendolyn.

"You are so thoughtful," she said kindly. "I can't remember anyone else bothering to ask how our fish are doing? I always knew you had a heart of gold."

# Chapter

## { 11 }

"GIVE ME BACK MY PICTURE!"

"What picture?" Stevie's face was innocent.

"The one you just took from my room."

"I didn't take anything."

"You did, too."

"I did not."

"Then what's that in your hand?" Cilla made a dive to retrieve her property, but only managed to get hold of his arm.

Quickly Stevie transferred the picture to his other hand. Then he pretended to drop it. Instinctively Cilla relaxed her grip and leaned forward. As soon as he was free, Steve dashed out into the hall and up the stairs, with his sister in hot pursuit.

From my vantage point on top of the bookcase, I watched them disappear. Half a second later came the sound of a crash, followed by an ear-piercing yell. This was followed by the slamming of a door, which made the whole house shake.

For the one hundred and fiftieth time, I wondered why those kids always had to make such a racket. It was a miracle I hadn't already had a nervous breakdown. I hoped fervently that the fight would be over before long. Right now I needed all the peace and quiet I could possibly get.

With my chin resting on the edge of my sleeping basket, I tried to pick up the train of thought that had been so rudely interrupted. The problem I had struggled with since this morning was this: What was happening to me?

For years I had spent practically all my time eating, sleeping, and socializing with the rest of the family. To have this familiar routine turned upside down was nerve shattering, to say the least. Lately, I had even had difficulty settling down to my daily naps. The whole affair was draining me of all energy, and I was beginning to feel like a zombie.

I was obsessed with the idea that Beethoven somehow was trying to take over my life. Now I asked myself again—was such a thing really possible? The thought was frightening.

Two nights ago, Beethoven had appeared in my

dreams again. He had worn a coat that was unbuttoned, knickers, and black shoes with large silver buckles. Extremely agitated, he had shouted something (presumably in German, since I hadn't understood a word) and waved his arms.

Last night he had reappeared. This time he was playing the piano. Ludwig I was in the dream, too, curled up in a chair nearby. Suddenly, right in the middle of a piece, Beethoven jumped up and began to shout again while walking back and forth, tugging at his hair.

What was the meaning of it all?

It was true that I resented the gradual infiltration of my life by my noble ancestor and his master. Yet, at the same time, I considered it to be my duty to fulfill whatever task it was that Beethoven wanted me to do. What was so frustrating was my inability to understand what he was trying to tell me.

I still had not been able to come up with a solution to my problems when, utterly exhausted, I finally managed to fall into a fitful sleep.

When I woke up again, the whole family was getting ready to go out to dinner. As I watched them leave, Stevie as usual being the first one out to the car, I breathed a sigh of relief. Hopefully they'd be gone at least a couple of hours. Lately I had learned to appreciate the little things in life, like having peace and quiet in the house.

· · ·

"Play!"

Although no sound was heard, there was no mistaking what Beethoven was saying. He was standing in front of me, hands clasped behind his back, the gray, bushy hair sprouting in all directions. Together with his carelessly tied cravat and the unbuttoned waistcoat, it gave him a wild and untamed appearance.

"Play!" Now he pointed a stubby finger in the direction of the piano.

Mesmerized, I stared at the instrument. Me, play the piano?

Anxious to escape this impossible demand, I instinctively took a step backward. Too late I discovered that instead of the floor there was only an empty void. Suddenly I found myself falling . . . and falling. . . .

I landed with a bump.

A sharp stab of pain shot through my body, and for a while I lay flat on my back, gasping for air. When at last I dared to raise my head, I found myself on the floor in the living room. The relief of being back in familiar surroundings was so overwhelming that I almost passed out. Thank goodness, it had only been another dream.

I vaguely remembered having curled up on the sofa with Cilla, while she and the rest of the family watched a late show after their dinner out. Judging by the gray daylight filtering through the curtains, it was now morning. The house was completely silent, which was not surprising. Even B. C. sleeps in on weekends.

For some reason the image of Beethoven was still amazingly real to me. Usually my dreams tend to fade away as soon as I wake up, but not this time.

"Anything wrong?"

Startled, I sprung to my feet. Winston was approaching from the kitchen. Silently he padded across the carpet, his protruding eyes heavy with sleep.

"Oh, it's you," I replied feebly. "I wish you wouldn't sneak up on me like that."

When he didn't answer, I babbled on. "Why should anything be wrong? I just woke up, that's all."

Winston stopped to gobble up a piece of glazed doughnut that someone had carelessly left behind. Swallowing noisily, he said, "Just wondering. The way you were stretched out flat on your back like a skinned rabbit, I thought you might be dead"—he chuckled—"or something."

"Oh, really!" Now my voice was frosty. "Well, I'm sorry to have disappointed you."

"That's okay," he said. "Better luck next time."

After grabbing hold of the blanket by the fireplace and dragging it closer to the heat register, he finally settled down.

"So," he said conversationally, "how are things?"

"What things?"

"You know. Ludwig and company."

Still sore from my fall, I moved over to the sheepskin rug, where I made myself as comfortable as possible.

Then, with a sigh, I said, "Now he wants me to play the piano."

"Who does? Ludwig?"

I shook my head. "Not him. Beethoven himself."

"Oh." He pondered this statement for a few moments. "I didn't know you knew how to play the piano."

"Of course I don't know how to play the piano." My voice was irritable. "What difference does that make? *He* doesn't care." After a moment I added bitterly, "Play! That's what he kept on saying. Play!"

"Did he say what he wanted you to play?"

Again, I shook my head. "He just told me to play, and then . . . well, then I woke up."

After that we were both silent for a while. As usual I kept on tugging absentmindedly at my hair until it was standing on end. Finally Winston spoke again.

"Well," he said. "Why don't you give it a try?"

"Give what a try?"

"The piano playing, of course."

"But I just told you I don't know how."

"How do you know you don't?"

"Of course, I know," I said impatiently. "Or have you seen me practicing lately?"

"But if you haven't even tried," he continued doggedly, "how do you know you can't play?"

"Well . . ." I began. Then I paused for a moment to digest what he had said. He might have something there. Maybe I did know. Maybe I was born with an exceptional musical talent. The more I thought about it, the more sense it made. After all, if Beethoven and Mozart could master the piano practically from infancy—why not me? If Beethoven were trying to take control of my life, maybe I had suddenly been infused with his genius.

"Maybe," Winston said eagerly, "this is how he wants to introduce his new composition. He'll make you play it and . . . uh . . . and. . . ."

"And what?"

". . . and. . . ." His eyes darted around the room until they fell on Mr. C.'s computer table. "That's it!" he exclaimed. His whole body trembled with excitement. "The tape recorder! Don't you see? He knows you don't know how to write music, so he wants you to record it instead."

I looked from Winston to Mr. C.'s cassette recorder and then back at Winston again. Gradually, a tingling sensation moved up my spine. Could it be true? Did I really dare to believe that I, the humble descendant of Ludwig I, had been chosen by the great composer himself as the instrument to bring to mankind yet another musical masterpiece?

My eyes moved over to the corner where the piano was. The lid was open as usual. Stevie always forgets to close it after he finishes practicing.

As if propelled by an unseen force, I now suddenly found myself on the piano bench, staring numbly at the keyboard. Winston was already standing on his hind legs with his paws on Mr. C.'s table, searching for the right button to push on the recorder.

"Well, old pal," he said after a moment. "Are you ready?"

My initial nervousness quickly dissipated as I reminded myself of the historic importance of the occasion. It wasn't exactly an everyday occurrence to have a brand-new work by one of the great masters come to light.

Already, I could see the headlines that would follow: 'WORLD STUNNED BY DISCOVERY OF NEW BEETHOVEN SYMPHONY. MASTERLY PERFORMANCE BY FELINE PIANO VIRTUOSO. DESCENDANT OF BEETHOVEN'S CAT, THE MUSICAL GENIUS OF THE CENTURY. . . .' I would, of course, be invited to appear on all the television talk shows, and—

"What's the matter, Wig . . . Ludwig? Too chicken to try?"

Annoyed as I was at having my train of thought interrupted, I refrained from giving the response his crude comment deserved. Without even turning around, I closed my eyes. "Quiet, please!" I murmured in a pained voice. "You're ruining my concentration."

I remained in this position for several moments. Then, with a dramatic and yet restrained movement, I raised my front paws until they hovered above the keys.

*"Tah!"* The sound was so soft I could barely hear it. Boldly, I pushed down another key, this time more firmly. *"Daah!"*

Encouraged by the result, I hit down again, using both paws at the same time. *"Taaa-daah!"*

Feeling the inspiration welling up inside me, I moved an octave higher before repeating the maneuver. *"Taaah-daaah! Taaah-daaah! Taah-daah-daaah!"*

Now I made a daring leap up onto the keyboard. *"TAH-DAHM!"*

I paused for a moment, savoring the sound that seemed to penetrate every fiber of my body. Next, giving my creativity free reign, I turned my attention exclusively to the black keys. *"Da-di-da-dah. Taa-dada-la-la-la-dida. Dadi-lala-ta-daah. Tah-dah-daaaaaaaaaaaaaa-aaaaaaaaaaaa. . . ."*

Somewhat disconcerted by the length of this last note, I looked down and discovered that my tail was stuck between two keys. With the disregard for personal discomfort that marks a true artist, I quickly freed myself.

Now a sudden urge came over me to express the enthusiasm and vitality that the great composer and I had in common. This led me to hammer furiously on the instrument, using the whole range of keys in a superbly inspired manner.

Absorbed as I was by my playing, I had nevertheless noticed a most peculiar behavior on Winston's part. He was alternately either jumping up and down or else waving his paws frantically in the air.

To be truthful, I was pleased with his reaction, which I assumed to be his way of showing approval of my

brilliant performance. Winston had never before displayed any interest in classical music.

I had now come to what I felt was the important *finale* of my masterpiece. For this I returned to the piano bench, from where I would play the finishing notes with the dramatic flourish they deserved.

Unfortunately, I was at that very moment whisked away from the piano by Mr. C., who held me in a vicelike grip that made my eyeballs pop and my ears hum.

In the silence that followed, I heard Winston's excited voice as if from far away. "I *warned* you, Wiggie. I *tried* to tell you that everybody was coming downstairs. Didn't you see me *wave* at you?"

# Chapter

# ❨ 12 ❩

IT WAS HALF AN HOUR LATER.

The whole family had gone back to bed. Steve had been duly reprimanded for leaving the piano open, and I had received a severe scolding from Cilla. Now I was curled up in my basket in the study, where Mr. C., with unnecessary force, if I may say so, had dumped me.

As a result of my recent activity, my legs and paws ached. I was hungrier than ever but I still had no desire to eat anything but fish. I was also bothered by a strange ringing sensation in my ears. Playing the piano had turned out to be a lot more demanding than I had expected. Adjusting myself to a less painful position, I now tried to think of a way to get some water to moisten my parched throat, without having to stir from my bed.

Winston, who had disappeared as soon as Mr. C.

showed up, had not yet returned. Josh was presumably out on an early-morning rendezvous with one of his feline friends. Since he had missed my brilliant performance, I was anxious for him to listen to the recording.

Probably because of my impaired hearing, I was blissfully ignorant of Winston's return until he suddenly bellowed, *"And how's the great concert pianist?"*

The effect of this unexpected outcry was electrifying. I sprang into the air like a jack-in-the-box, overturning my basket in the process. Breathing heavily, I stared in stupefaction at Winston's quivering jowls, which were only inches away from my face.

"What's the matter, old pal?" He licked his chops. "Cat got your tongue? I tried several times to get your attention but you seemed to have gone deaf, or something."

Judging by the numbness of my body, I figured my spine was probably broken, but since I have never been one to complain, all I did was whisper hoarsely, "Sorry. I guess I didn't hear you. I have this funny ringing noise in my ears." I made a feeble attempt to crawl back into bed, but the effort was too much. Instead I stretched out on the desk. "How did you like my performance?" I asked. "Pretty good, huh?"

"Your . . . uh. . . ." For some reason Winston looked uncomfortable. "Well, it was . . . eh. . . ." He squirmed and scratched his head. "It was very . . . uh . . . really, the way you played was . . . uh. . . ."

I knew exactly how he felt. Brilliant, stunning, inspiring—none of these expressions were adequate. Mere words were not sufficient to explain the masterful way I had handled that piano.

"Go ahead," I said modestly. "Say it. You never expected me to be able to play quite like that, did you? So"—I made an expressive gesture—"so powerfully?"

Winston looked relieved. "Eh . . . that's right. . . . Now that you mention it, you certainly put a lot of . . . of . . . *force* into your playing. Eh . . . force, and . . . and. . . ."

". . . feeling?" I suggested.

". . . uh . . . yeah, I guess so." He scratched his head again.

"Ah, well. . . ." I sighed with satisfaction. "When I think of the tremendous talent that had been buried inside me all these years, waiting to be discovered. And then, today. . . ."

For a moment we were both silent. Evidently, Winston was as overwhelmed by the experience as I was.

Unexpectedly, he chuckled. "You know, for a while there Mr. C. looked as if he was going to tear you to pieces, one limb at a time. That's when I decided to take a walk until things calmed down. Like they say, better safe than sorry."

Although disgusted by this unexpected admission of cowardice, I had to admit that Mr. C. had been pretty upset. If it hadn't been for Cilla, I might have found myself out in the cold for the remainder of the morning.

I shuddered at the thought. The last time this had happened had been the previous winter when I spent a dismal night huddled underneath the back porch.

I now decided to turn my attention to more pressing matters. "Would you mind bringing me some liquid refreshment from the kitchen?" I said. "I'm afraid the physical exertion during my performance has left me slightly incapacitated."

Winston blinked. Then he scratched his ear and looked puzzled. "Say, would you mind running that by me again?"

"Water," I murmured weakly.

It took a second for him to catch on. "You mean, you want a drink?"

I nodded.

"That's what I thought. You know something, Wiggie," he said earnestly. "It would be a lot easier if you used plain English instead of all these fancy words that you've been using more and more these days. Sometimes I get a headache just trying to figure out what you're talking about."

Not wanting to brag, I merely murmured, "Superior knowledge of our native language just happens to be another one of my inherited talents."

Winston chuckled again. "That was a pretty good workout you had, you know. Ha, ha, ha. After all, the only exercise you've ever known has been your trips to the kitchen for meals and going to the bathroom."

I frowned disapprovingly.

"Ever since the days of the Roman Empire," I said rebukingly, "mental exercise—the use of the brain—has been considered far more important than. . . ."

"Have you ever thought of jogging around the block in the morning?" he went on unheedingly. "Or maybe running up and down the stairs fifty times a day, or. . . ."

I finally lost my patience. "For your information," I said sharply, "I consider myself to be in excellent physical condition. However"—here I looked worriedly at my tummy—"I suspect I've lost at least a pound as a result of my piano debut."

"You have?" Winston suddenly perked up. For some reason he seemed to find this piece of news most interesting. "A pound, eh?" He eyed me speculatively. "Let me see now." Here he frowned and stared into space. "If you play the piano every morning for the next two weeks or so . . . and if you lose a pound each time. . . ." He cleared his throat in an attempt to prevent another outburst of hilarity. ". . . and if there's anything left of you after that . . . ha, ha . . . we'll give you a nice funeral. How's that, Wig . . . Ludwig?"

I still hadn't forgiven Winston when, late that afternoon, we finally had the house to ourselves. The whole family, including B. C., had gone out for pizza. Josh was dozing in front of the fire, and Winston was chomping away on a large ham bone that Mrs. C. had given him. As for myself, I felt somewhat better after my six-hour nap, although any movement of a sudden nature tended to result in pangs of discomfort that matched the hunger pangs that still gnawed at my stomach.

Peeking over the edge of my basket, I said to Winston, "Well, how about it?"

"How about what?"

"The recording of my piano performance," I reminded him.

"Oh. That."

I found this casual referral to Beethoven's latest work most annoying. Even someone like Winston, with his shallow cultural appreciation, should be able to understand the historical importance of what had taken place.

"You want me to play it?" he asked now.

"Please."

Having spent all day downstairs, I knew that no one had used the cassette recorder, so at least the tape was still in it. I waited impatiently while Winston—with obvious reluctance—left his bone and lumbered over to the desk.

Now, even Josh was wide awake. "This had better be good," he warned.

Winston must have rewound the tape too far, because at first a rather monotonous voice was heard delivering some kind of lecture. The subject eluded me completely since I once again had trouble with my hearing.

I rubbed my ears vigorously but the noise persisted.

The voice droned on for another couple of minutes. Then there was a short pause.

*"Tah!"*

Finally, here it was. I breathed a sigh of relief.

*"Daah!"*

I glanced at Josh, who was listening with his mouth open.

*"Taaah-daaah! Taaah-daaah! Taaah-daaah! Taah-daah-d. . . ."* It stopped abruptly.

I sat up in alarm. "What's the matter?"

Winston went over and checked. After a moment he cleared his throat and said, "Sorry, old pal." His voice was apologetic. "I'm afraid that's it. That was the end of the tape."

# Chapter
## { 13 }

"MOM, WIGGIE STILL WON'T EAT HIS DINNER. WHAT do you want me to do?" Cilla was hanging on the swinging door to the kitchen, looking bored. As usual, she was playing with her hair, twisting it around her finger.

Her question was completely drowned by the noise from the vacuum cleaner. The task of cleaning the living room carpet was becoming increasingly difficult for Mrs. C., thanks to the two-foot-tall robot that was zigzagging across the floor like a drunken sailor. No matter what direction she pushed the vacuum, the robot somehow managed to cross its path.

Finally, utterly exasperated, Mrs. C. turned off the vacuum cleaner. Placing her hands on her hips, she called sharply, "Stevie! You come down here right this minute and get that creature out of here!"

No answer.

"Stevie! I'm warning you!"

"I'm coming."

Cilla tried again to get her mother's attention. "Did you hear what I said, Mom? Wiggie still won't eat."

Now the robot walked right into the wall, where it stopped momentarily before attempting to climb up the wall.

Holding a hand to her forehead, Mrs. C. focused her attention with difficulty on her daughter.

"Did you say something?" Her voice was strained.

Patiently, Cilla repeated her statement.

"I just don't understand it," was the weary reply. "Wiggie has always loved canned food."

"Well, he's not eating. He's just sitting there."

Sighing deeply, Mrs. C. walked into the kitchen. "What's the matter, Wiggie-baby?" Her voice was filled with concern. "How come you're not eating?"

I looked at her dejectedly.

"Do you want me to open another can, Mom?"

"It probably won't do any good." She sounded doubtful. "Oh, well . . . try the creamed liver."

Liver? How about a can of sardines or a nice plump trout?

Now Steve wandered in, carrying the robot. The arms and legs were still moving.

"Oh, there you are," his mother said irritably. "It's about time. And for heaven's sake, turn that thing off."

"I can't." Steve popped his bubble gum. "After I programmed him, the remote control broke down."

Mrs. C. raised her eyes to the ceiling as if appealing to some higher power. She said evenly, "Why I ever let your father talk me into allowing that thing in the house, I'll never know."

Cilla put the can of creamed liver on the floor. I stared at it without interest.

"Wiggie's eyes look kind of glassy," Steve observed with satisfaction.

Listen, big mouth, so would yours if you hadn't eaten for almost a week. In fact, your eyes look kind of retarded all the time. And not only your eyes, either. Your whole face. . . .

Now Mrs. C. bent over and picked me up. Then she went over to the stove and poured herself a cup of coffee. "I wish I'd had the sense to take him to the vet this morning." Again, she sighed.

"Don't they have emergency hours?"

"I'm sure they do, but it's Thanksgiving tomorrow and I'd hate to. . . . We'll bring him in first thing Friday morning."

"Maybe he's on drugs," Stevie suggested.

"Who is?" Mrs. C. looked startled. "The vet?"

"Not him. Wiggie."

"Oh, for pete's sake!" Cilla exclaimed. "Your sense of humor is really warped, you know that?"

Ignoring her, Steve said innocently, "There is really no need to take him to the vet until after Christmas. As fat as he is, he'll easily survive until then."

Hanging limply over Mrs. C.'s arm, I turned my head and bared my teeth at him. In my weakened condition, it was an effort.

"What a terrible thing to say." Cilla eyed him indignantly. "Wiggie has already lost too much weight."

"I wish I knew what's wrong." Mrs. C. shook her head worriedly. "I just hope it's nothing serious."

"Maybe it's his teeth."

"I already thought of that. They seemed to be all right." She added after a moment, "It could be a virus of some kind."

Right then, even the prospect of being taken to the vet failed to make an impression on me. I felt dizzy and light-headed, and the ringing in my ears appeared to be getting worse.

As Josh had pointed out a couple of days ago, it probably had been the vibrations from the piano that had made Beethoven gradually lose his hearing. Now it was my turn. Because of my dedication to the arts, I had jeopardized my health. I wondered how long it would be before I was totally deaf. Weeks? Months? At the moment I didn't really care. All I wanted was to curl up somewhere and go to sleep.

That night again, I dreamed that I was swimming around in the giant aquarium. As on the previous occasion, fish of all shapes and sizes surrounded me, their round eyes staring unblinkingly ahead. Some passed so close to me that I could have touched them, but when I reached out they slipped effortlessly through my paws.

Frantically, I paddled around. Like before, Beethoven was egging me on. If I could catch just one? . . .

And that's when I saw the monster.

It was the size of a whale, and it was headed right toward me.

The eyes were like giant marbles, and the enormous mouth was wide open. I wanted desperately to get away from the horrifying sight, but before I had a chance to turn around, I was sucked into the darkness of the cavernous mouth. . . .

I woke up cold and shivering.

Thank goodness, I thought, it had only been a dream.

The remainder of the night I dozed fitfully. Deep

down, I was afraid that if I fell asleep again the dream would be back. Finally, just before dawn I stumbled out to the kitchen for a drink of water.

Having satisfied my thirst, I discovered to my surprise that the hunger pangs that had been with me for days were gone. Although this should somehow have been reassuring, it wasn't. Even in my befuddled state of mind, I realized that unless I started eating again, I wouldn't be around very much longer. . . .

And it was then that I remembered the aquarium at Gwendolyn's house.

# Chapter

## ❴ 14 ❵

I SHOULD HAVE GONE BACK TO BED, BUT, INSTEAD, forced by some inner compulsion, I headed for the pet door.

It was still completely dark outside. I stepped over a length of frozen garden hose, while carefully avoiding a puddle of water that had turned to ice overnight. The lawn, no longer green, was covered by patches of snow interspersed by tufts of yellow grass, some of which was coated with a thin layer of frost.

When I reached the fence that separated our yard from the Bowers's, I paused for a moment, impressed by the peace and tranquillity, such a marked contrast to the usual daytime hustle and bustle. I couldn't remember when last I had been on an outing this late at night. Probably not since the end of summer.

It was with a feeling of unreality that I crawled under the fence and continued across the yard toward the back door of the Bowers's home. In my semi-starved condition, I had not given any thought as to how I would gain access to the house, much less what would happen after that. I certainly couldn't count on Gwendolyn, who, as far as I knew, was sound asleep upstairs.

At the thought of Gwenny, I felt a momentary pang of guilt. What would she think if she saw me now? Even worse—what would she think if she knew that I was planning to steal Kathy's pet fish?

I stopped in front of the screen door.

Don't be a fool, Ludwig, I told myself sternly. You can still back out, you know. If you go through with this, Gwenny will never forgive you. Besides, stealing is a crime.

Nonsense, a voice inside me protested. Go ahead. Gwenny will never find out. No one will. You must have fish. You deserve fish.

But those fish are her friends.

*Friends?* Since when does a cat make friends with a fish?

They even have names—Peter, Paul, and Mary.

So what? Gwenny didn't name them, did she?

But they are part of her family.

Don't make me laugh! The only thing they are part of are the four food groups. Fish is a food, remember.

But, what if. . . .

No buts. Unlike us cats, fish were *meant* to be eaten.

Just imagine yourself biting into a juicy, delicious specimen, crunching the bones between your teeth. . . .

My mouth began to water.

Weak as I was, both mentally and physically, I momentarily closed my eyes and leaned against the screen door. For some reason it wasn't latched, and I practically fell headlong onto the porch.

"See?" said the voice. "They even left the door open for you."

"Maybe so, but this is just the porch. The door to the house is shut."

But it wasn't. Not quite.

With some difficulty I pushed it open.

After that, it only took me half a minute to proceed first through the mud room, across the kitchen into the dining room, down the hallway, and finally up the stairs.

I knew which room was Kathy's, since I had been up there a couple of times with Cilla. It was the second on the right. Very conveniently, the door to this room had also been left open.

"Notice that?" said the voice. "It's fate. It was meant to be."

Still I hesitated.

What, I wondered, would my noble ancestor, Ludwig I, have done in this situation?

It came somewhat as a shock when the voice inside me said, "And who do you think you're talking to?"

I should have known.

. . .

Once I was inside the door, I sat down to survey the premises.

Over by the left wall I could see the outline of the bed. Its occupant was completely buried under the blankets and, judging by the regular sound of breathing, sound asleep. If Kathy was anything like Cilla, nothing short of an earthquake would wake her up.

Right next to the bed was a night table with a reading lamp and a stack of magazines. Over in the corner in a bean-bag chair sat a huge, stuffed pink pig.

In front of the window on top of the table was the fish tank.

Half a second later I was sitting right next to the tank. There were three fish there all right, swimming aimlessly around. Two of them looked like twins, while the third one was smaller and of a lighter color. With their round, staring eyes, they reminded me unpleasantly of the monster in my dream.

I looked at the sheet of cardboard that acted as a lid for the tank. It had a number of small air holes and was held in place by a potted geranium.

One of the larger fish—Peter? or was it Paul?— swam up to where I was sitting. Only the glass separated us, as he stared at me with an open mouth and a vacant expression. For some reason he reminded me of Gwendolyn. His tail moved slowly back and forth.

Swallowing, I licked my chops.

Maybe, I thought, if I could push the cover back just a fraction. . . .

I got up on my hind legs and squeezed one front paw in under the cardboard. By wiggling the paw, I managed to move the sheet slightly off center, leaving a half-inch gap between it and the edge of the tank.

Feeling the excitement growing within me, I repeated my maneuver, this time in a different spot. Here the cover moved more easily, resulting in an opening about two inches wide.

Now all I had to do was to get up on top of the tank and reach down and. . . .

Without further hesitation, I leaped.

I landed on the cardboard sheet, only to feel it immediately give way under me. As I plunged into the water, I barely escaped being hit by a large, unidentified flying object that zipped past my head. Not until it hit the floor with a loud crash did I realize that it must have been the potted plant.

After that, the water closed over my head, completely muffling the sound of someone screaming.

*Chapter*

{ 15 }

I STAYED SUBMERGED FOR WHAT SEEMED LIKE AN
eternity. In reality, I guess it probably was only a few
seconds.

Not having been prepared for what would happen,
I had at first swallowed considerable amounts of water.
As soon as I was able to get my head above the surface
again, I managed to cough up some of it. The taste, by
the way, was rather unpleasant.

Sneezing and spluttering, I clawed at the now-soggy
cardboard that had failed to support me. Finally I
managed to get a foothold of sorts and keep myself from
going under again. Most of my body was still in the
water, but at least I could breathe freely.

I didn't know what had happened to the original

inhabitants of the tank, nor did I care to find out. After all, I thought peevishly, and, as I later admitted, unfairly, if it hadn't been for them I wouldn't have been in this mess in the first place.

Because I had been preoccupied with trying to prevent myself from drowning, I had so far failed to notice what was going on around me. The muffled scream I had heard while submerged continued to shatter the night but came to an abrupt halt when someone turned on the overhead light.

"Mother!" I recognized Mrs. Bowers's voice. "Mother, are you all right?"

"Burglars!" The quavering voice was unfamiliar to me. "Thieves!"

"Please, Mother, calm down. There is no one here."

"Murderers!"

"You must have had a nightmare." Mrs. Bowers's voice was firm. "Why don't you. . . . Oh, my God! The aquarium! There's something in the aquarium."

"Burglars! Call the police!"

The sound of doors opening and closing and more footsteps.

"Mom?" Kathy sounded breathless. "I heard a crash. What happened? Is Grandma all right?"

"Murderers!" The quavering voice became shrill. "I told you. They broke the window."

"Judy, what the devil's going on? Why is—"

"The tank—" Mrs. Bowers wailed. "There's an animal in the tank."

To my relief, someone finally lifted me out of the water.

"It's just Gwe . . . no, it isn't." There was puzzlement in Kathy's voice. "It's Wiggie!" She held me up in the air and stared closely at my face. I blinked and sneezed. Water was running liberally down my back and onto the carpet. "Is that really you, Wiggie?"

"Wiggie?"

"The Carter's cat. You've seen him before, Dad."

"My glasses. Will somebody give me my glasses?"

"Look, there's water all over the floor. I'll get a towel. . . . Henry, can you give Grandma her glasses?"

Soon I was wrapped in something soft and dry and rubbed briskly by Kathy. I was still wet and miserable, but I no longer felt like a drowned rat.

Mr. Bowers stood in his wrinkled pajamas, scratching his head. Now he asked, "Can someone please tell me what the neighbors' cat is doing in our house at four o'clock in the morning?"

Kathy dried the inside of my ears with a corner of the towel. "Don't look at me, Dad," she said defensively. "I didn't let him in."

"Well, then, who did?"

Mrs. Bowers deposited the soggy remnants of the cardboard into the wastebasket. "Good heavens," she said impatiently. "What difference does it make? He probably got in yesterday and then went to sleep some-where." She brushed a strand of hair out of her eyes. "Thank goodness the fish are all right."

Kathy's grandmother was struggling to get out of bed. She wore a long flannel nightgown and had funny little curlers in her hair. After adjusting her glasses, she said tartly. "It's lucky I don't have a bad heart. Things like this could kill you, you know." She fumbled to get her slippers on. "I don't know about you, but I'm going down for some coffee."

On her way to the door, she stopped and peered nearsightedly at me. "Funny-looking cats you have around here. Looks like a skunk." She laughed unexpectedly.

Kathy's father muttered, "Well, I'm going back to bed."

"Are you going to fill up the tank, Mom?" Kathy asked.

"Not now." Her mother stifled a yawn. "There's enough water there. They'll be all right until tomorrow . . . I mean today. Whenever I wake up again."

I hadn't even noticed that Gwendolyn had come in. She sat by the door, obviously trying to figure out what was going on. Now Kathy's mother was picking up the pieces of the broken flowerpot.

"Hello, Gwenny," I said bravely. "How are you?"

She jumped as if stung by a bee. Wrapped up as I was in the bath towel, there wasn't anything she could see, except maybe my ears. Now she stretched her neck and looked up at me. "Wiggie?" she said uncertainly.

"In person," I said, attempting a lightheartedness I didn't feel.

"Is that really you, Wiggie?"

I sneezed a couple of times. I didn't feel that great, to tell the truth. Maybe I was catching pneumonia.

"Wiggie?" she repeated for the third time.

"Don't you recognize me?" I asked.

I could tell her poor brain was working overtime. "Of course, I recognize you," she said. "But what are you doing here? And why are you all wet?"

"Well. . . ." I laughed feebly while trying to come up with a plausible explanation for my presence. "You see, I was walking in my sleep." I cleared my throat. "That's right. I've been doing that a lot lately. I wake up in the strangest places without knowing how I got there."

Gwenny frowned. "You mean you walked all the way over here in your sleep?"

"I guess so. Not that I remember any of it, of course," I added hastily.

"But how did you get so wet?"

"Oh, that?" I thought quickly. "Well, you see, when I woke up I was sitting on the table by the fish tank. I don't know about you, but it's kind of scary to open your eyes and look into the face of a fish. My instinctive reaction was to get away from it, so I jumped up on the tank. I didn't know the flowerpot was there, so I knocked it down and the lid slipped off and I fell into the water."

Gwenny's eyes grew round. "Oh, you poor thing," she exclaimed. "That must have been terrible. You could have drowned."

"Believe me"—I felt acutely sorry for myself—"I almost did."

"But what about the . . . oh, I see they're all right." She was looking at the aquarium where Peter, Paul, and Mary had resumed their endless rounds. None of them looked any worse for wear.

"I'd hate to see anything happen to them," Gwendolyn continued. "They are such sweet little creatures."

I let that pass. As far as I was concerned, I'd be happy if I never saw another fish—dead or alive—for the rest of my life.

## Chapter

## { 16 }

I SPENT THE REMAINDER OF THE NIGHT CURLED UP beside Gwendolyn in the sewing room.

Kathy brought me home after breakfast. When she had finished explaining what had happened, Mr. C. said, in a tone of disbelief, "Well, if that doesn't beat everything." He stared at me as if I had suddenly dropped in from outer space. "Craziest thing I've ever heard of."

Mrs. C. said helplessly, "I just don't understand what's gotten into Wiggie lately. First, he stops eating—and now this. He's never acted this way before."

"Too bad he didn't drown," Steve said regretfully. He was trying to fix the remote control to his robot. The robot was lying on the floor, its legs jerking occasionally. "We could have had a nice funeral." Looking sideways at his sister, he added meaningly, "A real *Thanks* giving funeral. Get it?"

Cilla threw a magazine at him. "Don't you dare talk about Wiggie like that." She hugged me protectively. "Poor baby, he probably got lost in the dark and didn't know where he was."

"How could he get lost?" Steve continued to poke inside the mechanism with his screwdriver. "Cats don't get lost. They can see in the dark."

The robot made a final, spasmodical movement before going dead. It lay immobile on its back, with one leg sticking up in the air.

"Talking about funerals," Cilla said now. "Why don't you bury that stupid robot? It's broken, anyway."

"It's not," Steve protested. "I've almost figured out what's wrong. All I have to do is fix it."

"I bet," Cilla said scornfully. She put me down on the floor. "Let's go upstairs, Kathy. I've got a new record I want you to hear."

I retired to the kitchen, with Josh and Winston tagging close behind.

Josh's eyes were large as saucers. "Let's hear it, old pal," he said. "You mean, you actually jumped into the fish tank?"

"We-ell . . ." I replied cautiously. I rubbed my ears, which were bothering me again. "Not exactly."

"What do you mean, not exactly? Did you or didn't you?"

For a moment, I debated with myself how much I could safely divulge without deviating too much from the story I'd already told Gwendolyn.

But before I had a chance to speak, Winston said, "What I want to know is what you were doing over there at that hour in the first place?" He guffawed. "Having a romantic midnight rendezvous with Gwenny, eh?" He winked slyly at me.

With a disapproving frown, I said, "Of course not. Whatever gave you that idea? For your information, Gwenny didn't even know I was there."

"Really?" It was obvious that he didn't believe me. "And why were you there?"

While trying to come up with a suitable answer, I started cleaning my paws. A faint odor of fish was still clinging to my coat, as a reminder of my unfortunate adventure.

"It's rather obvious why he was there," Josh drawled. "He was catching a fish for dinner. He's been talking about nothing but fish recently, especially after you two heard Mr. C. talking about Beethoven feeding his cat fish."

I interrupted my grooming to give him a cold stare. "That's a totally unfounded accusation," I said. "I wouldn't dream of touching their fish." I paused. "If you really want to know the truth, I was sleepwalking. When I woke up I found myself in Kathy's room."

"Sleepwalking?"

"Sleepwalking?" Winston echoed.

"That's right." I sighed deeply. "I never told you this, but it's not the first time it has happened. The difference was that last night I found myself eye to eye with a fish. I was so startled that, without even stopping to think, I jumped up on top of the tank. How was I to know that all that covered it was a piece of flimsy cardboard? So you see," I finished self-righteously, "the whole thing was just an accident."

Josh and Winston regarded me in silence.

Finally Josh said, "You mean that's really how it happened? Scout's honor?"

"Scout's honor."

Actually, I was rather proud of the dedicated manner in which I had ventured outside in the middle of the night. With complete disregard for my own personal comfort and safety, I had responded to the promptings of my noble ancestor and his master. Even though, due to circumstances beyond my control, I was prevented from completing my mission, I nevertheless felt that I had done my part.

Having lost all desire for fish, I forced myself to eat some of the Thanksgiving turkey. To my surprise, it only took a few measly mouthfuls to make me feel stuffed. My stomach must have shrunk—or something.

The next morning found me in the waiting room of the vet clinic. Unfortunately, there were no other patients ahead of me, and before long I was whisked inside.

"And what have we here?" Dr. Matson asked with disgusting cheerfulness, after dumping me on the cold and slippery examination table. "Oh, my." He clucked his tongue. "We do look a little bit under the weather, don't we?"

We? I glared at him. Speak for yourself, dummy. I don't know about you but considering my recent experiences I'm doing pretty well, thank you.

"And what seems to be the problem?"

While Mrs. C. recapitulated the history of my life, Dr. Matson pinched and prodded and squeezed me until I was black and blue. If I hadn't been sick before, I was sure to be after he was done with me.

Next he pulled down my eyelids until my eyeballs threatened to fall out, shone a flashlight inside my ears, and pushed a popsicle stick down my throat until I gagged. I tried my best to throw up on his hand, but unfortunately I didn't have enough time.

After all that, he took my temperature—a procedure I hate more than anything else—and checked my weight. Although my temperature was normal, it turned out that I had lost over three pounds since my last visit.

"Of course," Dr. Matson said in a soothing voice, "in this case, the weight loss really doesn't matter since Wiggie always has had an obesity problem."

I tried unsuccessfully to dig my front fangs into his arm. Unfortunately, he managed to evade the maneuver by having his assistant pin me to the table.

"As a matter of fact," he continued, "he could easily lose another pound and still be of normal weight for his size."

When Mrs. C. made some protesting noises on my behalf, the vet whisked out a syringe from somewhere. Before I had a chance to brace myself, he plunged the needle into my side.

"Protein," he announced briskly. Then, after refilling the syringe, "Multivitamin." Another refill. "B-12."

The last shot must have hit a bone or nerve or something, because it practically paralyzed me. While trying to wriggle myself free from the iron grip that held me down, I succumbed to an urge to sneeze. All too late, I discovered my mistake.

"Ahaa!" A fiendish smile appeared on Dr. Matson's face. "Your nocturnal bath has not proved to be very beneficial to your health, has it?" Gloating, he made preparations for yet another injection. "We don't want to risk getting pneumonia, do we?"

And why not? Feel free to have as much pneumonia as you want.

"Antibiotics," he explained to Mrs. C., as he pulled the needle out. "As they say, better to be safe than sorry."

Really? Well, one more shot, and we'll see who is sorry.

As we passed through the waiting room on our way out, a large, vicious-looking animal was stretched out on the floor. He looked like a cross between a wolf and a Great Dane.

My spirits rose. The dog looked like he might, without much provocation, chew Dr. Matson to pieces. Too bad I wouldn't be around to watch it.

*Chapter*

**⟨ 17 ⟩**

MUCH TO MY RELIEF, THE REMAINDER OF THE Thanksgiving holiday was uneventful. A sudden blizzard, accompanied by freezing temperatures, kept everybody indoors. Even Winston, much to his chagrin, was forced to forgo his daily neighborhood excursions.

Mr. C. took a break from the work on his dissertation to play chess with Stevie and peek-a-boo with B. C. Most of the time, however, he was stretched out on the living room couch, sleeping, his face covered by a newspaper.

That was the case late Sunday afternoon when the phone suddenly rang.

"Will somebody get that?" Mrs. C. was in the bathroom getting B. C. cleaned up. Somehow he had managed to unscrew the top of his bottle, dumping the formula all over himself. I really had to hand it to him. That child is a genius.

The phone kept on ringing. Peeking over the edge of my basket, I could see that Mr. C. was still fast asleep.

"Will somebody please answer the phone!"

Mr. C. still didn't stir.

Now Mrs. C., carrying the dripping-wet baby, hurried into the kitchen to answer. Mr. C. changed position, causing the newspaper to slide down on the floor. Yawning, he opened his eyes and sat up.

When his wife came in a moment later, she commented dryly, "I see you're finally awake. Honestly, I don't understand how you can sleep all day."

Mr. C. looked hurt. "I was not sleeping," he protested. "I was reading the newspaper."

"Really?" She grabbed a towel from the rack inside the bathroom door and wrapped it around B. C. "Then why didn't you answer the phone?"

"The phone?" He looked startled. "Eh . . . I guess I was too wrapped up in the sports page."

"Maybe you should see a doctor. There's definitely something wrong with a person who snores as loud as you do while reading. Here." She handed him the baby. "This should help to keep you awake."

Mrs. C. had temporarily abandoned her Finnish studies and was for a few days indulging in her favorite pastime—murder stories. Earlier in the week she had checked out a stack of books from the public library.

As usual, she was reading four different books at the same time. Whenever she had things to do in the kitchen, she managed to read snatches of *Death of a Murderer.* During her sometimes very lengthy visits to the bathroom, she enjoyed *You Can't Kill Them All.* Next to her favorite chair in the living room was *They Died by Accident,* while *Occupation: Murder* kept her from going to sleep at night.

As far as Cilla and Steve were concerned, they were enjoying one of their infrequent periods of truce. On these occasions they managed to occupy themselves, either separately or together, without a single fight or argument or even as much as a snide remark. As a result, the atmosphere in the Carter household was one of rare peace and tranquillity.

Personally, I was trying to get some much needed rest. My daytime naps were relatively uninterrupted, but at night I continued to be hounded by Beethoven and my illustrious ancestor. Understandably, after the recent unfortunate fish incident, my feelings toward Ludwig I were not exactly friendly.

The difference between my present dreams and those I had had earlier was that now neither my ancestor nor Beethoven made a sound. In spite of this, it was obvious that Beethoven was trying to convey a message of some kind. His lips were moving and, as always, he was very agitated, but not a word was heard. At first I assumed that the great composer was expressing his displeasure over my failure to get his symphony recorded. Now, I was not so sure. His gestures somehow indicated that he wanted me to put a stop to something. But what? It was very frustrating, to say the least.

I also found the fact that I was unable to hear anything very disturbing. Was this an indication of things to come? Would I, too, one day become completely deaf? It was a frightening prospect.

Because of all this, my nights continued to be anything but restful. A feeling of permanent exhaustion prevented me from any strenuous activities, and I spent practically all day curled up in my basket.

Although I dutifully showed up in the kitchen at mealtimes, I had no real appetite. I only ate enough to keep Mrs. C. happy and thus avoid the possibility of another visit to the vet clinic.

I knew, of course, that my pals were worried about me. More than once I had caught them discussing my case when they thought I wasn't overhearing their conversation.

"Listen, Wig . . . Ludwig," Josh said, as I passed through the kitchen after a routine visit to the backyard, "you really have to snap out of this thing, you know. The whole situation is ridiculous. You can't go on letting those two characters ruin your life."

"What am I supposed to do?" I asked dully. "They won't let me alone."

"But don't you realize that they are dead?"

"So?" I shrugged helplessly.

"I know," Winston said jokingly. "You could use exorcism to get rid of them. Like they do with evil spirits. Ha, ha."

Josh snickered.

"That's all right," I said bitterly. "Go ahead and have your fun. You're not the one who never gets enough sleep. You're not the one who is heading toward a nervous breakdown from trying to figure out what it is they want you to do."

I was interrupted by Cilla, who came strolling into the kitchen carrying her pocket recorder, as usual turned up at maximum volume. She was playing her favorite rock music. Humming to herself, she took a can of soda from the refrigerator and returned upstairs.

Josh, who had kept his ears covered with his paws, drew a sigh of relief. "If Beethoven wasn't already dead," he commented, "he'd probably commit suicide if he had to listen to stuff like that."

Silently, I agreed. The only kind of music that Cilla and Steve ever listened to was rock, and, evidently, they thought that the louder it was, the better it sounded.

Winston sat with his mouth open, staring into space. I recognized the signs. Evidently, he was having one of his infrequent brainstorms. Slowly, he came out of his trance and focused his eyes on me. "That's it," he said eagerly. "Don't you see? That's what they want you to do."

"What?"

"Get rid of the rock music, of course."

I stared at him.

"Well?" he continued somewhat impatiently. "Say something. What do you think? Couldn't that be it?"

"You think they want me to get rid of the rock music," I repeated, to make sure I got it right.

He nodded.

"Just like that, huh?"

Again he nodded.

"I see." I looked at the familiar face with the bulging eyes and protruding jaw. He seemed completely serious.

"And just what do you propose that I should do?"

"Well . . . I don't know." He scratched his belly. "Make them stop playing it, I guess."

I looked from him to Josh.

"Don't look at me," Josh said quickly. "It wasn't my idea."

Returning my attention to Winston, I said sarcastically, "And what exactly did you have in mind? Should I schedule a lecture tour across the country, stressing the evil influence of rock music on today's society? Or should I be a little more drastic and plant bombs in all the radio stations that play rock? Or. . . ."

"I don't think you understand," Winston interrupted. "I wasn't talking about the whole country. I was talking about this house. Here. Us."

I had to admit that this made more sense. To make

Cilla and Steve give up rock should be a more manage-
able project than trying to change the whole world. Seen
in that perspective, Winston might even be right.

"Well?"

"I'll think about it," I said.

# Chapter

## ⁅ 18 ⁆

THE MORE I THOUGHT ABOUT WINSTON'S SUGGES-
tion, the more I liked it, especially since I didn't have a
single idea of my own. It certainly made sense to assume
that the musical atmosphere in our household might be
offensive to someone like Beethoven.

Of course, not even Beethoven could complain
about Mr. C.'s taste. While doing his research, Mr. C.
likes to listen to one or the other of Beethoven's many
symphonies. Another favorite of his is the violin con-
certo.

As far as Mrs. C. is concerned, whenever she wants
a break from Finnish, she'll either put on a Mozart tape
or turn on the radio for some light popular music.

That left (as I had expected) Cilla and Stevie as
culprits and sole targets for my operation.

"If you need any help," Winston said, licking his chops in anticipation, "I'll be happy to nip Steve's ankles whenever he turns on the stereo."

I shook my head. "That's too obvious. You do that a few times, and you'll be taken you-know-where." (I was counting on the remote possibility that Dr. Matson had avoided being chewed up by that vicious-looking dog.) "You might even end up at the dog pound. Besides, this is something I have to do myself." I tugged absentmindedly at my hair, remembering again, with pride, who I was. "I'm going to use a more subtle approach."

"Like what?"

"I don't know yet," I confessed, "but don't worry, I'll think of something."

For some reason I had never before noticed how cluttered the house was with devices capable of producing music.

Just in the kitchen alone were a radio, a portable TV, and a cassette recorder. The living room had a stereo system, a TV, a VCR, a CD player, and another cassette recorder. Then there was the clock radio and the television in the master bedroom, and Steve's room—with its three record players (two of which were broken), two radios, a TV, and a Walkman. Cilla had in her bedroom a stereo, a miniature TV set, and a cassette player. Even B. C. had his own little tape recorder.

"It's simply ridiculous," I exclaimed to Josh, after

we had finished going through the house. "They've got enough stuff between them to open up a store."

Josh nodded in agreement. "It must have cost them a pretty penny."

"And what's more," I continued, "they don't even need half of it."

"Well," Josh said philosophically, "I guess we should consider ourselves fortunate to live in such an affluent household. . . ."

"But that's just it," I said earnestly. "If they are that anxious to throw their money around, why can't they have a new pet door installed? Or buy one of those fancy litter boxes with the electronic air cleaner?"

Josh sighed wistfully. "That sure would be nice," he agreed. "Susie has one of those."

"You see?" I said gloomily. "That goes to prove my point. I bet we're the only cats left in the neighborhood who still have to go outside."

It wasn't too difficult to locate the two main sources of rock music in the house. One was the stack of cassette tapes that Cilla kept on her desk. She played these non-stop whenever she was home. The other was the supply of rock videos that she and Steve never seemed to get tired of watching.

The videos all seemed to be more or less the same, featuring weird-looking characters with yellow or green or purple hair (some of them actually had no hair at all) and clothes that no normal human being would dream of wearing. Most of the performers looked as if they rightly belonged in an insane asylum.

Josh and I were curled up on the rug in front of the fireplace watching Steve, who was watching the same video for the third time in a row.

"I can certainly sympathize with Beethoven," Josh murmured. "I don't see how anyone has the nerve to call that horrible noise music, anyway." He started cleaning his whiskers. "By the way, have you come up with any bright ideas yet?"

"Just wait," I said smugly.

As I had expected, Steve soon went into the kitchen to look for something to eat. That kid puts away more food than anyone else in the family. Not that it shows, of course. He is still thin as a reed.

I gave Josh a nudge. "Watch this."

In a flash, I was up on the glass table that held the VCR. I leaned against the control buttons on the front panel and rubbed my body back and forth a couple of times. Immediately, the picture on the screen became fuzzy and the blaring sound of the rock band ceased abruptly. Now all that could be heard was the hissing sound as the tape was beginning to rewind.

By the time Steve reappeared, holding a sandwich in one hand and a glass in the other, I was back on the rug, licking my paws and yawning discreetly.

"Hey!" Steve came to a halt. "What's going on? Who's been fooling around with the video?" He looked around the living room, which—not counting Josh and me—was empty.

For a moment he seemed puzzled. Then he went out into the hall and yelled, "You'd better not pull any more stuff like that, or you'll be sorry. . . ."

I suppressed a snicker. "Cilla isn't even home," I said to Josh. "She's still at her tennis lesson."

Satisfied that his threat had had the desired effect, Steve started the tape all over again and, munching on his sandwich, resumed his watching.

About ten minutes later, the phone rang.

"I'll get it." Steve headed for the kitchen, bumping into at least three pieces of furniture on the way. While he was gone, I repeated my performance.

This time he was gone long enough for the recorder to complete rewinding the tape and turn itself off.

Steve's jaw dropped at the sight of the blank screen. "What the . . .?" he began. Then he turned around and ran upstairs. Doors were opened and slammed shut again. "It's no use hiding," he yelled. "I know you're there. . . ."

It was another few minutes before he gave up and returned downstairs. A moment later, the front door flew open and Cilla and Kathy made a noisy entrance, accompanied by a blast of cold air.

When Steve heard them, he jumped up from the couch and sauntered out into the hall with his hands in his pockets. "You guys think you're so smart, huh?" he said.

Cilla, who was unzipping her coat, gave him a blank look.

"You thought I didn't hear you go out, huh? Well, I did." He gave a fake laugh. "You can't fool me, you know. No, siree."

Kathy raised her eyebrows in Cilla's direction.

"Don't pay any attention to him," Cilla advised. "He was born weird."

"Go ahead. Play innocent," Steve continued. "But just wait until I tell Dad. He'll probably never let you use the VCR again."

Cilla pulled her boots off and kicked them under the bench. "Listen," she said, "I don't know what you're talking about and I couldn't care less. Why don't you leave us alone and go on upstairs and play with your toys?" She patted him on the head. "Come on, Kathy."

Later during dinner, Steve had even less luck convincing his parents that Cilla had played tricks on him.

"There's probably something wrong with the video player," his father said reasonably. He helped himself to a generous portion of lasagna. "After all, we've had it for—how long now? Five years?" He looked around the table.

"Six," Mrs. C. corrected him. "It's time we got a more up-to-date model, anyway."

"Goody." Cilla's face lit up. "Then can I have the old one for my room?"

*Another* VCR? My head started aching at the thought.

Suddenly overcome by the futility of my self-appointed task, I retired to my basket on top of the bookcase. There I stared listlessly at the picture of my two forebears.

"Do me a favor, will you," I mumbled tiredly, "and go and pick on somebody else for a change."

But as usual they robbed me of my nightly rest. I didn't realize that I was tossing and turning and crying out in my sleep until Winston finally woke me up.

"Do you have to make such a racket?" he grumbled irritably. "It's only two in the morning, you know."

Peeking over the edge of my basket, I said apologetically, "Sorry, old pal. I didn't mean to wake you up."

The remainder of the night I lay on my back, staring into the dark. It was true that I was proud of my noble heritage and the trust that both Beethoven and his cat had placed in me. At the same time, however, their constant interference in my life and their incessant demands were making me miserable. With all my heart, I wished that I could return to my former carefree existence. I knew I couldn't go on like this much longer.

The next morning, feeling more dead than alive, I nibbled halfheartedly on my breakfast. The sound of rock music from Cilla's room did nothing to improve my temper.

Josh had already cleaned his bowl. "What do you intend to do about that?" he asked, pointing at the ceiling.

It was at that very moment that the events of the past several weeks suddenly seemed to converge and come to a head.

Overcome by a sudden rage that literally made me see red, I raced out of the kitchen and up the stairs to Cilla's room. With a gigantic, flying leap, which startled Cilla into dropping her curling iron, I landed on her desk. As luck would have it, I skidded right into the stack of cassette tapes, scattering them all over the floor.

I looked wildly around for the cassette recorder, only to discover that it was right under my nose. By clawing furiously at it, I managed first to dislodge the cord, causing the music to come to an abrupt end. Then, with a herculean effort, I pushed the recorder itself off the desk and into the wastebasket.

Surprised by the sudden attack, Cilla stood as if rooted to the floor. She stared at me with eyes that were as large as saucers, a stunned expression on her face. Shocked into immobility by the sudden violence of my own actions, I stared back at her. For what seemed to be an eternity, neither of us moved. Then all of a sudden, Cilla came to life again.

"Help!" She flung the bedroom door open. "Help, somebody! Wiggie has gone crazy!"

# Chapter

# { 19 }

NO ONE SPOKE DURING THE DRIVE TO THE VET clinic.

Mr. C., who had been forced to push aside his research because of me, was concentrating on trying to avoid the many patches of black ice that made driving treacherous in the afternoon traffic.

I was sitting in Cilla's lap, securely wrapped in a quilted baby blanket that had been Steve's. A gray cat with a pink ribbon around its neck was appliquéd to the front. The blanket was now mine but was only used for special occasions, like on my birthday or during the Christmas holidays.

A few times when I had been really sick and had had to stay in Cilla's room, she had also let me use it. I was glad she had remembered it today. It made me feel a little better. After all, I thought sadly, it wasn't every day that your favorite cat showed signs of cracking up.

Miserable as I was, I couldn't help speculating over what kind of treatment the vet might consider necessary this time. Probably another batch of shots, at the very least.

Suddenly I was struck by an alarming thought. What if Dr. Matson diagnosed me as being dangerous? Would he recommend that I be dumped at the animal shelter? or—the alternative was so frightening that I instinctively buried my face in the blanket—would he insist that I be put to sleep?

With a pang of regret, I recalled the countless occasions when I had tried to dig my teeth into his arms. Would he hold that against me now? Some people—and he looked like he might be one of them—never miss an opportunity to get even.

I also remembered the time when I had chased one of his patients around the waiting room, accidentally knocking down a potted cactus and a display rack with pamphlets, in the process. Not to mention the time I scratched the receptionist when she tried to take back the ballpoint pen I was playing with—she had at least half a dozen other pens in a cup on her desk, but of course she had to have mine.

And then, unfortunately, there had been the memorable day when I tried to avoid having my temperature taken by escaping to the top of a cabinet. I had thought at the time that they were making too much fuss over nothing. After all, how was I to know that they kept glass bottles of rubbing alcohol stashed away up there?

There was only one other patient in the waiting room—a puppy who was about to get his baby shots—so once again it was my turn only a few minutes after our arrival.

Dr. Matson chewed absentmindedly on his glasses while listening to Mr. C.'s explanation of the reason for our visit. Then he went through his usual routine of pushing and prodding and checking my temperature, after which he extracted some blood.

As soon as he was done, Cilla gathered me up in her arms again. I leaned my head gratefully against her shoulder, wondering what would happen next. Dr. Matson was unusually silent, which I took as a bad sign.

"I'm afraid this case is a little outside my field," he said finally. "While there is nothing physically wrong with Wiggie, he is obviously a very disturbed cat. There-fore"—he wrote something on a note pad—"I am refer-ring him to a colleague of mine who specializes in mental and emotional disorders." He tore off the page and handed it to Mr. C.

Ignoring the paper, Mr. C. said, in a tone of in-credulity, "You mean, Wiggie needs a *psychiatrist*?"

Dr. Matson nodded affirmatively. "That's right.

And I can highly recommend Dr. Malone. She has a rare insight into the many complex things that might be troubling an animal."

Due to my lethargic condition and the constant ringing in my ears, it took a few seconds for the word "psychiatrist" to sink into my brain. When it finally did, I instinctively made a flying tackle in Dr. Matson's direction. Unfortunately, he chose that particular moment to turn around, and I only managed to dig my claws into the back of his white coat. I remained in this precarious position for several seconds, clinging to the fabric of the coat, until I was forcibly removed by Mr. C. After that, I had to confine myself to hissing and waving my paws threateningly in the air.

"Obviously, Wiggie's condition is deteriorating rapidly." Dr. Matson eyed me rather coolly while adjusting his coat. "The sooner you can get him under Dr. Malone's care, the better."

Cilla asked curiously, "Does Dr. Malone treat people *and* animals?"

The vet chuckled. "I'll have to tell her that one. No, of course not. She is a licensed veterinarian who specializes in psychiatry. She only treats animals."

Cilla seemed impressed. "Gee," she said, "I didn't even know there was such a thing as an animal psychiatrist."

"Oh, yes," Dr. Matson said breezily. "There is a specialist for everything, nowadays. As a matter of fact, a friend of mine who graduated from vet school recently is now a podiatrist." When Cilla looked puzzled, he explained: "A podiatrist specializes in foot care. Or, in this case"—he chuckled again—"paw care."

I was still seething with righteous indignation as we left the vet clinic. If there was anyone around here who needed to see a shrink, it was Dr. Matson. With a shudder, I recalled the expression of gloating on his face whenever he was giving me a shot. The man was dangerous, I realized now. Definitely dangerous.

During the drive to the psychiatrist's office, I made two unsuccessful attempts to wiggle out of Cilla's lap. When that didn't work, I pretended I had gone to sleep. Then, as soon as Mr. C. had parked the car and Cilla was reaching for the door handle, I made a daring leap over her shoulder to the back of the car, where I quickly crawled under the seat.

As I lay there, surrounded by old candy wrappers, shriveled-up apple cores, and some kind of gooey substance that was sticking unpleasantly to my whiskers, I was reminded of the last time I had taken cover under this very same car seat. Admittedly, that had been several years ago, but I remembered clearly that I had been able to turn completely around and even roll over on my back.

Now, when I tried to squeeze in just a little farther, I couldn't. Already I was so firmly wedged in that I was unable to move. I reflected for a moment over the undoubtedly inferior construction that must have been the reason for the excessive sagging of the seat. As Mr. C. always said, they sure didn't build cars the way they used to. Due to the manner in which my head was flattened between the bottom of the seat and the floor, I hardly dared to breathe, for fear that my brain would come oozing out through my ears.

Someone must have opened the rear door, because I felt a sudden rush of cold air.

Then I heard Cilla's stern voice. "And just what do you think you are going to accomplish by acting like this, Wiggie? You look perfectly ridiculous with your head under the seat and the rest of your body sticking out. How did you ever think you could hide under there, as plump and fat as you are?"

Stung by her remark, I made a cautious attempt to wiggle my hips. She seemed to be right insofar as only my head and my front paws were wedged under the seat. Before I had a chance to extract myself from my uncomfortable position, I was unceremoniously dragged out and whisked inside the building, with the blanket wrapped so tightly around my body that I must have looked like an Egyptian mummy.

Dr. Malone's waiting room, which strongly resembled the one at the vet clinic, was empty. For lack of anything else to do, I found myself staring at an abstract painting on the wall, which depicted a cat with two heads,

six legs, and three tails. Closer scrutiny, which left me slightly cross-eyed, opened up the possibility that maybe it was two cats instead of one. Or was it two and a half? Either way, it was definitely strange.

My cultural appreciation was interrupted by a door opening at the other end of the room. A large woman, with a Pekingese clutched to her ample bosom, emerged. After pausing for a moment to give us a hostile glance, she sailed across the room like an oversized battleship headed for war. The Pekingese, whose eyes were slightly glassy, burst into unexpected laughter as they passed us.

*"Ha, ha, ha, hi, hii-ii"*—here he almost choked— *"ho, ho, ha, ha, ha, ha.* Going in for your session, are you, dearie? *Ha, ha, ha,* well, good luck . . . *hi, hi, hi. . . ."* The door slammed behind them, cutting short his outburst.

A cold chill went up my spine. What kind of place was this, anyway? Frightened, I hid my face in Cilla's jacket, wishing I was a hundred miles away.

# Chapter

## 〔 20 〕

THERE WAS A MOMENTARY SILENCE FOLLOWING THE battleship's departure. Then Cilla said, "What do you think Dr. Malone will do with Wiggie, Dad?"

Mr. C., who was leafing through a magazine, responded dryly, "Have him lie down on a couch, I guess, and tell her about his childhood."

Cilla giggled. "You hear that, Wiggie?" She rubbed my nose. "Maybe you're doing these weird things because your mother box-trained you too early—or something."

Her remark led me to wonder what Dr. Malone might want to know about my past life. Come to think of it, I had seen enough psychiatrists in action on television to be familiar with the procedure. All they seemed to do, anyway, was ask a lot of questions. Things like "Did you hate your mother?" They always made it seem abnormal if you didn't. If you didn't hate your father, either, then it was definitely something wrong with you. "Did you feel repressed as a child?" "Did you ever wish your teacher would drop dead during class?" "Did you ever . . ."

"But seriously, Dad, what do you think she'll do?"

Mr. C. stifled a yawn. "I'm afraid, I don't have the slightest idea. Frankly"—he gave me a resentful look— "I'm more concerned about what our neighbors will say when they find out that I took my cat to a psychiatrist."

Dr. Malone turned out to be a slender woman in her thirties, with dark hair and a pleasant smile. After scratching my ear and talking to me for a moment in her soft voice, she took me out of Cilla's arms.

Still wrapped in my blanket, I sat in her lap while she was talking to Mr. C. and Cilla. I could tell she knew how to handle cats, because she gave me time to make myself comfortable and then left me alone.

After a few preliminary questions about my age and health and things like that, she asked, "When did you first notice a change in Wiggie's behavior?"

Cilla and her father looked at each other.

"I guess when he went over to the neighbors' in the middle of the night and almost drowned in the fish tank," Mr. C. said.

To Dr. Malone's credit, she didn't even smile. "That must have been an upsetting experience for him," she commented gravely.

"But it started long before that," Cilla protested. "He stopped eating, remember?"

"Oh, yeah." Mr. C. scratched his chin. "That's right. . . . I had forgotten."

". . . and before that he was just lying around all day."

"When, approximately, was that?" Dr. Malone asked.

Now Cilla leaned forward in her chair. "I just remembered something else," she said eagerly. "One morning I found Wiggie on the floor, trapped underneath his basket. Somebody must have knocked it down off the bookcase while he was sleeping. Maybe he hit his head or something when he fell down, and maybe. . . ."

My eyelids had been getting increasingly heavy, and at that point in the conversation, I finally fell asleep. I didn't wake up again until Dr. Malone rose from her chair.

"Well," she rubbed my ears, "I think that might well have been how it all started. . . ."

Mr. C. said protestingly, "But it's just a *picture,* for goodness sake. Wiggie doesn't understand. . . . He's only a cat, remember? The drawing could have been of a . . . a hippopotamus, and he wouldn't have known the difference."

It took me a few seconds to figure out what they were talking about. When I finally did, I was really hurt by Mr. C.'s lack of faith in me. Did he think I had suddenly become so retarded that I couldn't tell the difference between a hippo and a cat? I might be going deaf, but I still had perfect vision.

"Why don't you let me be the judge of that?" Dr. Malone said pleasantly, but firmly. She handed me back to Cilla. "If you would be so kind and drive over to the public library and check out any book they might have on the subject of political cartoons, I would appreciate it. I'm sure you know what I'm referring to. They're the kind that appear daily on the editorial pages of newspapers."

I could tell that Mr. C. wasn't too thrilled about the whole thing, but before he could make any objections, Dr. Malone said persuasively, "It really would save us all a lot of time. Also"—her eyes twinkled—"it might prevent you from having to come back here another day."

When Mr. C. returned with the book she had requested, Dr. Malone banished him and Cilla to the waiting room. Then she put me down on the floor.

"Now, Wiggie," she said briskly, "you and I are going to look at some funny drawings called political cartoons." She kneeled on the floor and opened the book. It was both large and heavy, reminding me of the old world atlas in Mr. C.'s study.

"You look like a very intelligent cat," she continued

(too bad Mr. C. wasn't around to hear that), "and I'm counting on you to understand what I'm going to tell you."

She kept on turning the pages. "As soon as I heard how you had been acting, I knew what your problem was. Of course," she added, "I might be wrong, but. . . ." She left the sentence unfinished.

Looking up, a mischievous smile unexpectedly spread across her face. "You really tried to catch those fish, didn't you?"

Stung by the question, I stared haughtily back at her. Me, steal fish? That's a pretty serious accusation, lady. If you go around saying things like that, you could get yourself into a lot of trouble.

"To eat, I mean?" She winked at me.

*Well!* What exactly did she think I was? Some kind of cannibal? She'd better watch it, or I might sue her for defamation of character. Didn't she know that my motto has always been Live and Let Live? That I had even. . . .

"Poor Wiggie!" Now she picked me up and cradled me in her arms. "You've been through quite an ordeal, haven't you?"

Have I ever? I sighed. Boy, I was sure glad she had *some* understanding of my problems.

". . . but it just won't do to sneak over to the neighbors' in the middle of the night and try to kill their pet fish."

I sat up with a jerk. I hadn't come here just to get insulted.

"If everybody would go around trespassing on other people's property and helping themselves to whatever they wanted without permission, then the world would. . . ."

What did she mean, trespassing? Didn't she know that the Bowers's were my bosom buddies? And that Gwendolyn was like a sister to me? For your information, lady, I can go over there any old time I want, and besides, if people don't even bother to lock their doors at night, then . . .

"Let me see now." Turning somewhat more professional, Dr. Malone pulled out a plump, round cushion from under her desk. "Why don't you lie down here"— she plopped me down right in the middle of it—"and we'll take a look at the book."

Well—this was more like it. I decided to leave the looking to her, while I rolled over on my back and relaxed. It only took me a few seconds to discover that I wasn't resting on an ordinary cat bed. No, siree, this was an honest-to-goodness genuine water bed. Gingerly, I wiggled my hips. The bed moved softly up and down. Wow! How come we didn't have one of these at home? I'd have to get Cilla to come in and see it before we left. . . .

". . . and I want you to understand that just because there is a strong resemblance between you and Beethoven's cat, that doesn't necessarily mean that. . . ."

Happily, I adjusted my rear end to a more comfortable position while preparing myself for the questions that were sure to come. Too bad, I thought regretfully, that my childhood had been so uneventful. I pondered this unfortunate circumstance for a few moments. I could, of course, bring up the fact that my parents had failed to recognize the early signs of my genius. Not that I was going to hold that against them. Nothing could be farther from my mind. No—after all, one of the burdens of greatness was to be misunderstood by the rest of the world.

"And now. . . ." Dr. Malone raised her voice an octave, causing me to reluctantly open my eyes. After making sure that she had my full attention, she propped the book up in front of me. "If you look at this drawing . . ." she began.

# Chapter
## ⁅ 21 ⁆

AS SOON AS WE CAME HOME, CILLA CARRIED ME UP TO her room. Carefully she put me down in the basket on top of the dresser. Then she tucked the cat blanket around me. Within a matter of seconds I was fast asleep.

When I opened my eyes the next morning, I felt like a new person. It was amazing what a good night's sleep could do. Still without stirring, I looked out the window. It was snowing again, large, fluffy flakes that were falling softly to the ground.

I suddenly became aware of the silence in the house. Usually mornings were pretty noisy. Where was everybody? It was then I also realized that the constant ringing in my ears had ceased. It had been with me almost continuously since my piano performance. Now, for the first time, my hearing was back to normal. It was a great relief.

I climbed out of my bed and did a few brief stretching exercises before jumping down onto the floor. Then I went out into the hall. For a moment I stopped and listened. No, not a sound anywhere. As I passed Steve's room I took a peek inside. No one there, either, and the bed unmade as usual. Good heavens, was it really that late? Had everyone left already?

When I came down to the kitchen, Josh greeted me from the top of the refrigerator. That's his latest hangout. Mrs. C. has thoughtfully removed the empty canning jars she used to keep there and provided an old bath towel for him to lie on.

"Well, if it isn't the great Ludwig himself," he said now. "How did it go yesterday? I hear you had to see the shrink. What did he say?"

Refusing to rise to the bait, I concentrated on my breakfast, which this morning had remnants of someone's scrambled eggs added to it. Probably Cilla's, I decided. Usually she remembers her diet when she has practically finished eating.

The food tasted unusually good. For so long now, my appetite hadn't been what it used to be, and I was pleased to feel the gastric juices stirring again. Meticulously, I licked the bowl clean, after which I rinsed the food down with some milk. Then I began attending to my morning toilette. Josh was still stretched out on his towel. His head was hanging over the edge of the refrigerator.

"Well," he said again. "What did he say?"

I looked briefly at him before continuing my grooming. "Doctor Malone—who, for your information, happens to be a woman—said that I was the victim of a misunderstanding," I explained. "Whoever made that drawing deliberately exaggerated the likeness between Beethoven and his cat. In fact, there was probably no likeness at all." I paused before continuing. "As far as Ludwig I is concerned, however, there is no doubt that I am indeed his direct descendant." Actually, what Dr. Malone had said was that Ludwig I belonged to a breed that was very common in those days and that I was simply a throwback, but I wasn't about to tell Josh this.

Josh's mouth fell open. "You mean, that's all?" He sounded disappointed.

I nodded. "That's all."

For a minute we were both silent. Then Josh said, "So your name is Ludwig because his name was Ludwig?

I shrugged. "That's right. As I said earlier, it has obviously been passed on from father to son for countless generations. It's just part of my noble heritage. As for the reincarnation theory, Dr. Malone said I had an exceedingly active imagination. But then, of course," I added with suitable modesty, "this often goes along with a brilliant mind."

There was another silence while Josh tried to digest this.

"But how did the shrink know?" he asked finally. "About the drawing, I mean?"

"Well," I explained, "she had a book that had hun-

dreds of similar drawings in it." I chuckled to myself.
"You should have seen some of them. I haven't laughed
that much in a long time. There was, for example, a
cartoon that showed President Kennedy looking like a
donkey. Or a donkey looking like President Kennedy,
whichever you prefer. And then there was Franklin D.
Roosevelt looking like a horse. And. . . ." I stopped as
I suddenly remembered Mr. C.'s putting the book down
on the living room table. "Come on, I'll show you."

Josh landed on the floor with a thud. Together we
continued into the living room. To my surprise, Winston
was there, deeply engrossed in the cartoon book. For
some obscure reason, he had Mr. C.'s marking pen in his
mouth.

When he saw us, he dropped the pen. "Oh, hi,
there, Ludwig. Glad to see you finally woke up. For a
while this morning, everybody thought you had died in
your sleep. Ha, ha."

"Ha, ha," I said dryly. "Very funny. And while I
remember, allow me to inform you that my name is
Wiggie."

Winston stared dumbly at me with his bulging eyes.
"Huh? Say that again."

"I said that my name is Wiggie. Not Ludwig."

He picked up the pen again, moving it to the corner
of his mouth. "I see." It was obvious that he didn't.
"What happened?"

I took a deep breath. "I have just come to a decision,
that's all. I'm no longer affiliated with Ludwig van Bee-

thoven, the famous composer. Even though Ludwig I is my honorable ancestor and I have his blue blood in my veins, I've decided to just be myself." I bowed my head to indicate that, in spite of my proud heritage, I was willing to count myself as one of the humble masses. "Which," I added, "is why I prefer to be called Wiggie."

Winston still didn't look as if he understood, but finally he said, "Sure thing. That's fine with me. I always liked Wiggie better, anyway."

"And now," I said, reaching for the book, "if you'll excuse me, there are a few things I want to show Josh. . . ."

Winston stepped back. "Wait a sec," he said suddenly. He adjusted the marking pen between his teeth. "Look at me. Who do I remind you of?"

Josh and I both stared blankly at him.

"Come on, come on," he said impatiently. "Don't I remind you of somebody? Somebody famous?"

We kept on staring. After a moment, Josh said uncertainly, "Your mother?"

"My *mother?* Since when is *she* famous? Look"—he pointed at the pen—"this is supposed to be a cigar. Get it? Now, who do I remind you of?"

Josh and I first looked at each other. Then we looked at Winston again. Finally Josh said brightly, "A dog smoking cigars?"

"A . . . for pete's sake," he groaned. "What's the matter with you guys? Haven't you ever heard of Winston Churchill? The great British statesman? Can't you see that I'm the spitting image of him? Look, I'll show you." He placed his paw on the open book and started turning the pages roughly. "See this?" He stopped at one of the pictures. "That's a bulldog, right? And what am I? A bulldog. Now, notice the face of this bulldog. It's Winston Churchill's face. And have you noticed the name . . . Winston. Get it? Let me tell you guys, it's destiny. No wonder I always felt out of place here. Deep inside my heart, there was a kind of. . . ."

Josh and I escaped to the kitchen. Winston didn't even notice.

"Well," I said after a while, "I guess it happens to the best of us."

"I guess so."

"Is that how I used to act?"

"More or less." Josh shrugged diplomatically.

For the next few minutes, we pondered the situation in companionable silence. Absentmindedly, Josh started grooming his tail.

"Well," I said finally, "let's look at the bright side. Maybe Dr. Malone has some kind of family rate. . . ."